He was called Smith and he was twelve years old. He was a pickpocket—and a good one at that—in the grimy, shadow-filled underworld of eighteenth-century London. The place he called home—a dingy cellar in a disreputable tavern—was shared by his two sisters, who made their living altering the clothes of hanged men.

Leon Garfield has made this unlikely figure the hero of his new book and has assembled a supporting cast of equally unlikely characters: among them two shady, scurrying men in brown; the gallant highwayman Lord Tom; a blind judge; a hangman; and the prisoners of Newgate Jail. And every one of them is involved with a document and—a murder.

The reviewers of Mr. Garfield's first two books, JACK HOLBORN and DEVIL-IN-THE-FOG, amply support our claim that this young British writer is a master storyteller with invention, originality, wit, and a magnificent feeling for the language and flavor of the eighteenth century.

HE WAS called Smith and he was twelve years old. He was a pickpocket—and a good one at that—in the grimy, shadow-filled underworld of eighteenth-century London. The place he called home—a dingy cellar in a disreputable tavern—was shared with his two sisters, who made their living altering the clothes of hanged men.

Leon Garfield has made this unlikely figure the hero of his new book and has assembled a supporting cast of equally unlikely characters: among them two shady, scurrying men in brown; the gallant highwayman Lord Tom; a blind judge; a hangman; and the prisoners of Newgate Jail, and every one of them involved with a document and a—murder.

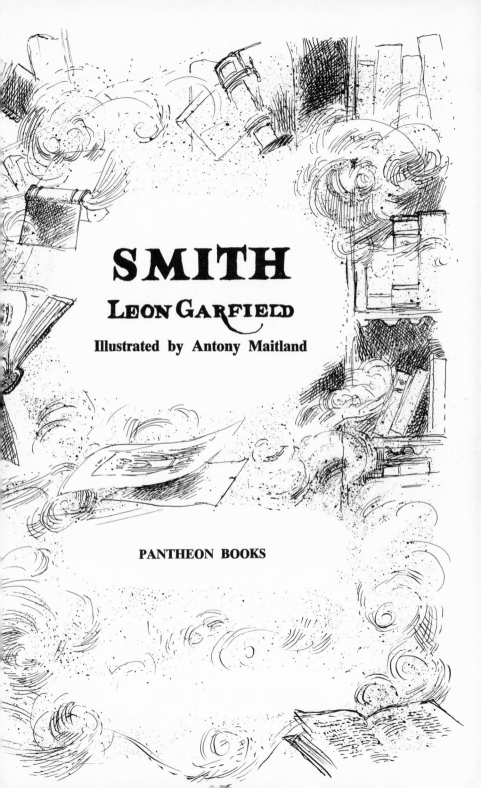

SMITH

Leon Garfield

Illustrated by Antony Maitland

PANTHEON BOOKS

To
my brother

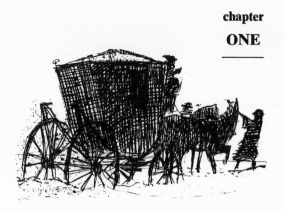

HE WAS CALLED "Smith" and was twelve years old. Which in itself was a marvel: for it seemed as if the smallpox, the consumption, brainfever, jailfever, and even the hangman's rope had given him a wide berth for fear of catching something. Or else they weren't quick enough. For Smith had a turn of speed that was remarkable, and a neatness in nipping down an alley or vanishing in a court that had to be seen to be believed. Not that it was often seen: for Smith was rather a sooty spirit of the violent and ramshackle Town, and inhabited the tumble-down mazes about fat St. Paul's like the strong smells and jaundiced air itself. A rat was like a snail beside Smith, and the most his thousand or more victims ever got of him was the powerful whiff of his passing and a cold draft in their dexterously emptied pockets. Only the sanctimonious birds that perched on the Church's dome ever saw Smith's progress entire. As their beady eyes followed him, they chattered savagely, "*Pick*pocket! *Pick*pocket! Jug him! Jug-jug-jug him!" as if they'd been appointed by the Town to save it from such as Smith.

His favorite spot was Ludgate Hill, where the world's coaches, chairs, and curricles were met and locked, from morning to night, in a horrible, blasphemous confusion. And here, in one or other of the ancient doorways, he leaned and grinned while the shouting and the cursing and the scraping and the raging went endlessly, hopelessly, on. Till, sooner or later, something prosperous would come his way.

At about half past ten of a cold December morning an old gentleman got furiously out of his carriage (in which he'd been trapped for an hour), shook his red fist at his helpless coachman and the roaring but motionless world in general, and began to stump up Ludgate Hill.

("*Pick*pocket! *Pick*pocket!" shrieked the cathedral birds in a fury.)

A country gentleman, judging by his complexion, his clean, old-fashioned coat, and his broad legged, lumbering walk which bumped out his pockets in a manner most provoking.

(Smith twitched his nose and nipped neatly along like a shadow . . .)

The old man's pace was variable: sometimes it was brisk for his years, then he would slow down, hesitate, look about him as if London had changed much since last he'd visited, and he was now no longer confident of his way. He took one turning, then another: stopped, scratched the crisp edge of his wig, then eyed the sallow, seedy city gentry as if to ask the way: till he spied another turn, nodded, briskly took it—and came straight back into Ludgate Hill.

An ancient fellow with a face like the wind had blown its nose on it, eased out of a doorway as if to accost the old man. But did not. He'd glimpsed Smith. Looks had been exchanged, shoulders shrugged—and the old villain gave way to the young one.

On went the old gentleman, confident now of his bearings, but deeper and deeper into the musty, tottering forest of the Town where Smith hunted fastest and best.

Now a sharpish wind sprang up, and the cathedral birds eyed the leaden sky (which looked too thick and heavy to admit them), screeched, and flew to the lower eminence of the Old Bailey courthouse. Here, they set up a terrific commotion with their legal brethren, till both Church and Law became absorbed in watching the progress of Smith.

"*Pick*pocket! *Pick*pocket! Jug-jug-jug him!"

The old gentleman was very deep in Smith's country now, and paused many a time to peer down the shambling lanes and alleys. Then he'd shake his head vaguely and touch at his coat pocket—as if a queer, deep sense had warned him of a pair of sharp eyes fairly cutting into the cloth like scissors. At last, he saw something familiar: some landmark he'd remembered. Godliman Street. Yes: he was on Godliman Street . . .

As suddenly as it had sprung up, the wind died—and the cathedral birds flew back to their dome.

"*Pick*pocket! *Pick*pocket!"

The old gentleman began to stump very particularly down Godliman Street, eyeing the old, crumbly houses that were lived in by God knew how many quiet, mysterious souls. And as he went his shadow seemed to divide—into itself and a thin, cautious, second shadow that was not so much seen as sensed . . .

For this was the deepest heart of Smith's forest (hidden even from the cathedral birds), where he hunted at his pleasure—there being no other in his small, dark life. Here, the houses reared and clustered as if to shut out the sky and so promote the growth of the flat, pale, and unhealthy moonfaces of the clerks and scriveners, glimpsed in their dark caves through dusty windows, silent and intent.

Came a slit between two such properties, a quiet way roofed over at first floor level: Curtis Alley, leading to Curtis Court.

Framed by the darkness of its alley, Curtis Court presented a gray and peaceful brightness—a neglected clearing in the forest of the Town where nothing grew, and all save one of the enclosed houses had had their eyes put out with bricks—on account of the tax.

As the old gentleman's steps echoed in the alley, a solitary, dusty raven flew up out of the court with a bitter croak. Suddenly, the old gentleman gave an involuntary shudder, as if someone or something had swiftly passed him by—and thereby made a draft.

"Someone's walked over me grave!" he muttered, shook his head, and entered Curtis Court.

"Beg pardon, sir! Beg pardon—"

Out of a doorway on the left of the court came Smith. Which was the first time the old man had ever laid eyes on him: though all the way from Ludgate Hill there'd never been more than two yards between them!

He stopped, flustered, about six paces from the end of the alley. Which way was the damned urchin a-going? This way? That way? Angrily, he shifted, and Smith, with a quaint clumsiness, brushed against him, and . . .

It was done! In an instant Smith had emptied the old gentleman's pocket of—

He halted. His eyes glittered sharply. Footsteps in the alley! It would be blocked! He changed direction as briefly as a speck in the wind—and vanished back into his doorway! So quickly had this been done that, seconds after he'd disappeared, the old gentleman was still staggering and bewildered.

Out of the alley came two men in brown. Curious fellows of a very particular aspect: whom Smith knew well. Uneasily he scowled—and wished he might vanish through the crumbling bricks.

The old gentleman had recovered himself. He stared round angrily, till courtesy got the better of him.

"Good day to ye, gentlemen!" he said, with an apologetic smile.

The newcomers glanced quickly across the court toward the house that had kept one window, and grinned . . .

"And good day to *you*!"

They moved very neat—and with no commotion. They were proficient in their trade. The taller came at the old man from the front; the other took on his back. And slid a knife into it!

The old gentleman's face was fatefully turned toward a certain dark doorway. He seemed to peer very anxiously round the heavy shoulder of the man who was holding him—as if for a better view. His eyes flickered with pain at the knife's quick prick. Then he looked surprised—amazed even—as he felt the cold blade slip into his heart.

"Oh! Oh! Oh my . . . " he murmured, gave a long sigh—and died.

His last sight on this earth had been of a small, wild, and despairing face whose flooded eyes shone out of the shadows with all the dread and pity they were capable of.

For Smith was only twelve and, hangings apart, had seen no more than three men murdered in all his life.

They say that murdered men's eyes keep the image of their last sight for—for how long? And do they take it, hereafter, up to the Seat of Judgment? Smith shivered. He'd no wish for his face to be shown in any place of judgment—in this world or the next!

In a terror as violent as his dislike, he watched the two men in brown. He'd be pleased to attend *their* hanging. Even if he had to pay for a place!

They were dragging the luckless old gentleman toward

the darkness of the alley. (Why hadn't he stayed in the country where he'd belonged? What business had he to come stumping—so stupid and defenseless—into Smith's secret forest?)

Now Smith could hear the quick, fumbling sounds of searching. Methodical gentry. Still no commotion. Ho, they knew what they were at! But the sounds grew harsh and hasty. Even irritable.

Muttered one, "God rot the old fool! He ain't got it!" (Got what?)

Came a new sound. A very queer one. A tapping, limping, scraping sound—as of a lame man's footsteps on the cobbles. Then a soft, gentlemanly voice:

"Well?"

"Nothing . . . nothing, yer honor!"

"Liars! Fools! Look again!"

Again, the sounds of searching—accompanied by strained, indrawn breath.

"Told you so. Nothing."

A groan. A very dreadful affair—that seemed to come more from the bowels of the Town than from any human lips.

"Again! Look again! It *must* be there!"

"Well, it ain't, yer honor! And if we stays much longer, we'll be on our way to join 'im—on the end of a rope! Come—let's be off!"

"Again! Search once more!"

"With respect—do it yerself, sir!"

"No!"

"Then we're off! Quick! Quick! There's someone coming. Quick."

There was a scuffling and scraping, then the alley and court were momentarily quiet. A shadow crossed the broken, moss-piped paving. It was the raven, making ready to return.

But Smith did not move yet. Voices and clustering footsteps could be heard coming from the far side of the alley. Somehow or other, the pale faced clerks and scriveners and thin-necked attorneys had caught the scent of spilt blood. They'd come out of their rooms and chambers to congregate solemnly—and stare.

(Yet no one came out of the houses within the court; not even from the house with the single window. Strange . . . strange . . .)

Now the crowd had grown and oozed into the court itself. The raven flapped sourly up to a gable and creaked with a sardonic air: for Smith had invisibly joined the outskirts of the crowd, muttering away with the best of them: then was through, like a needle through shoddy, to Godliman Street and beyond!

(As he went, a door opened in the court, and some one came palely out . . .)

A quarter mile off, on the other side of St. Paul's, Smith stopped running. He sat on some steps and fumbled in his ragged, ancient coat. What had he got this time? Something valuable. Something that had been worth the old gentleman's life.

He fished it out. A document. A *document*? Smith stood up, swore, spat, and cursed. For, though he was quicker than a rat, sharper than a stoat, foxier than a fox; though he knew the Town's corners and alleys and courts and byways better then he knew his own heart; and though he could vanish into the thick air in the twinkling of an eye, he lacked one neccessary quality for the circumstance in hand. He could not read. Not so much as a word!

DARKNESS CAME PREMATURELY to the Town, owing to the sun's habit of vanishing into the tall chimney pots of Hanover Square—where, for all Smith knew, it blazed away in the rich parlors till the time came for it to be trundled off to Wapping and begin its course anew.

By four o'clock, the dome of St. Paul's stood black and surly against the darkening sky, and its huge shadow was flung eastward, over the narrow streets and lanes of that part of the Town.

At last, Smith gave up his efforts to force the cramped and awkward ink lines to yield up their secret. For the light was gone and his eyes, wits, and soul were aching

with strain. . . . A hundred stratagems had presented themselves to him—and a hundred stratagems he'd rejected.
He'd thought of applying to the various scholars of his
acquaintance—but which one could he trust? He'd
thought of cutting the document into its various lines—or
even words—and giving each of them to a different
reader. But what if he muddled the order, or lost something that proved to be vital?

He walked; he sat; he tramped as far as the churchyard
on Old Street, where he leaned up against a headstone,
puffed at his short clay pipe, and fished out the document
yet again. He stared; he screwed up his eyes and face till
he looked like an old walnut, but the dim air and his own
dark ignorance made the document seem like the last will
and testament of a very old, very lame, very inky spider—
on its weary way home.

So Smith likewise, with a deep sigh, packed up his
thoughts and went home.

Between Saffron Hill and Turnmill Street stood—or,
rather, slouched—the "Red Lion Tavern." A very evil-
looking, tumbledown structure, weatherboarded on three
sides and bounded on the fourth by the great Fleet Ditch
which stank and gurgled and gurgled and stank by day
and night, like the parlor of the Tavern itself.

This parlor was an ill-lit, smoky, noxious place, full of
hoarse secrets and red-eyed morsels—not so much from
all walks, as from all falls of life. Thieves, pickpockets,
footpads, unlucky swindlers, and ruined gamblers boozed
and snoozed here, and were presided over by a greasy
landlord who never sold a customer to the gallows for less
than a guinea.

Here was Smith's home. Not in the dignity of the parlor

itself, but in the cellar below it, where he lodged with his sisters, Miss Bridget and Miss Fanny.

"Not nubbed yet?" remarked the landlord humorously, as Smith humped broodily in.

Smith, his head full of darker things than even the "Red Lion Tavern," made no answer.

"I spoke to you, Smith."

"Did you now! I thought it was a belch from the old Ditch!"

Two or three customers grinned, and Smith dodged deftly past the landlord to the cellar steps. But was not quite quick enough to miss a fist on his ear. He howled and vanished . . . and the landlord laughed fit to burst.

"Got him that time!"

"You asked for it! You brought it on yourself!" remarked Miss Bridget, looking up from stitching a brown velveteen coat.

"Poor little Smut!" murmured Miss Fanny, over a pair of gray breeches. "One day he'll come down them steps stone dead!"

"*I'm* not complaining," said Smith, rubbing his ear which, had it been clean, would have been red as a strawberry, but instead, was now a warm black. "Saw an old gent done in today."

"Indeed? And what's that to do with abusing the landlord?"

"Me mind was on other things."

" 'Tis no excuse! We brung you up to be genteel. Fanny and me feels the disgrace."

"Put a dab of vinegar on your little lug, Smut," said Miss Fanny. " 'Twill take out the sting."

She mentioned vinegar as there was a quantity of it in the cellar: for the sisters engaged in scouring and cleaning, beside making genteel alterations to cast-off clothing from unfortunates who were hanged and so never had a chance to wear out their last garments. The velveteen coat and the gray breeches were bespoken by the hangman himself, for they'd come off a very high-stepping rogue indeed—one everybody was sorry to see nubbed.

"But the law must take its course," had said Miss Bridget. And, " 'Tis an ill wind," had said Miss Fanny, when Smith had brought in the garments . . .

"Look what I got this time!" said Smith, after he'd wiped his ear with vinegar. He fished out the document and spread it on the table, full in the light of the tallows. "Just before he was done in. Not a quarter of a minute!"

The Smith family stared at the document. None of them could read.

"What is it?" asked Miss Fanny.

" 'Twas what he was killed for," said Smith, and went on to relate exactly all the circumstances of the crime, not forgetting the unseen man with the limp, the thought of whom terrified him more than anything else.

"It's a deed to property," declared Miss Bridget. "For that queer thing" (she jabbed her needle at a piece of writing) "that looks so like a horse and cart, is the word 'property.' Indeed it is. I'd know it anywhere!"

Smith was not convinced.

"Then why was he done in for it? And why was they so frantic when they couldn't find it? Poor old fool!"

"Reasons," said Miss Bridget somberly, and returned to the velveteen coat. "Reasons."

"I think," said Miss Fanny, "that it's a confession, or an accusation. For that's the sort of thing a murder's done for—excepting money: and it ain't money. Now—though I don't quarrel with Brid's 'property,' for I believe her to be right, there's a 'whereas,' most distinct: and that piece like a nest of maggots, there," (she pricked with her needle) "I *know* to be 'felonious.' Oh yes, indeed, Smut, dear: you got a confession which will be very valuable if we can only find out what's been done. For, if they was willing and able to kill for it—well, they'll be equal willing to *pay* for it! Clever Smut!"

Smith frowned, still not convinced, but inclined more to a confession then a property deed. But, in his heart of hearts, he thought the document might be something else altogether: but he said nothing, having nothing to go on, nor any piece of knowledge to contradict his sisters with.

"So we must get it read out to us," continued Miss Fanny, neglecting the breeches, "so we can know where to apply."

"And who, miss, would you ask?" queried Miss Bridget, irritably.

"Lord Tom can read," said Smith, thinking of his highwayman idol and friend.

"Lord Tom?" repeated Miss Fanny, blushing and smiling. "The very scholar!"

Miss Bridget sneered. "That highwayman is so much in his cups, his mouth's grown like a spout! Mark my words, miss, I'd as soon trust him with anything worth money as I'd trust the landlord! Not that I think the paper's worth money at all: for it's neither more nor less than a deed to property!"

They went on arguing thus till the tallows burned low: with Miss Bridget inclining more and more to property, and Miss Fanny, who was softer and younger (being scarce nineteen), keeping to the romantic notion of a confession on whose value as blackmail they might all live happily ever after. But on one thing they were all agreed: the difficulty of finding someone they could trust enough to read it to them.

Then, when the room was full of tallow smoke and shifting shadows, Miss Bridget and Miss Fanny retired to their curtained-off bedroom, and Smith to his corner in the workroom itself.

For some minutes one tallow remained alight, and afforded Smith a somber view of the brown velveteen coat and the gray breeches bespoken by the hangman. They were upon a hook in a corner and presented a disagreeable resemblance to their aspect when their late owner had last worn them. Smith wondered if he was likely to come back for them, fearful white and moaning about the cold. Well—they'd not fit him now!

He screwed up his face scornfully at the thought of ghosts but continued to stare into dark corners till he fell asleep; and, when he awoke, did so with a startled air and looked about him with some relief to see the old brick and plaster walls and the dim gray daylight falling down the cellar steps . . . as if his dreams had given him cause to doubt his firm belief in no ghosts.

The document was still on the table. He folded it up and began to tiptoe toward the stairs . . .

"Where are you off to, Smut, dear?"

Miss Fanny, much tousled and creased, had poked her head through the curtain.

"Newgate," said Smith, briefly. "Got business."

"What are you going to do with our dockiment, Smut?"

"Don't know—yet."

"Wouldn't it be safer here?"

"Why?"

"Well, dear—if them that wanted it did in an old man for it, they won't think twice about doing in a boy!"

"Don't know I got it! Never saw me! There's only you and Miss Bridget what knows."

"Oh yes . . . that's true. But you never can tell, Smut. *Someone* may have seen you. Won't you leave it behind?"

"No."

"Are you going to show it to Lord Tom?"

"Don't know. Maybe."

"If he's going to Newgate," came Miss Bridget's voice, still croaked with sleep, "tell him to screw some money out of that Mister Jones, for there'll not be another stitch done till there's something on account! 'angmen is horrible customers! So degrading!"

Miss Fanny's head, which had vanished for the moment, reappeared.

"Mister Jones, Smut. Brid says see Mister Jones." Then she sighed. "For the last time, dear—leave the dockiment behind. 'Twill be safe as houses. Oh Smut! I've an 'orrible feeling you was seen and are in danger! Oh Smut! I fear you'll be coming down them steps tonight stone dead!"

A TREMENDOUS IDEA had lodged itself in Smith's mind: and, like all truly great things, answered its purpose so exactly that one exclaimed, "Why hasn't it been thought of before?" He would *learn* to read!

The morning was dull and windy. The cathedral birds were huddled upon Old Bailey, which stood to the leeward side of the stench from Newgate Jail. Such merchants and clerks and attorneys who walked the whipping streets kept their heads down and their hands to their wigs and hats— as if to hold their darkly aspiring thoughts from flying out to become common property. A general frown and scowl creased their faces: another day was bad enough, without the insolent wind aggravating it!

Smith had spread the document inside his coat and across his chest, where it kept him from the worst of the weather.

"Be still, old fellow," he muttered from time to time as the stiff paper pricked and tickled. "You and me's got business. You and me's going up in the world . . . just as soon as I gets you to talk!"

He was crossing Ludgate Hill when suddenly he fancied he saw the murdered old gentleman, stumping along ahead of him. He stopped, much frightened. Then he looked again and saw the old gentleman was someone else altogether. But thereafter, the murdered man stayed pretty firmly in his thoughts—as if keeping a watch on his document and where Smith was taking it.

Which, in the first place, was to the blackened and gloomy felonage of Newgate Jail. Smith turned in at the Lodge, greeted the jailer there, and lit up his battered pipe against the dreadful smells to come.

First, he sought out Mr. Jones, the hangman: a short, stout, hornyhanded gent whose hair shone with pomatum. He got three shillings out of him on account—together with a surly prophecy that if he, Smith, didn't mind his P's and Q's he'd become Mr. Jones's customer in a transaction with a yardage of hemp.

"P's and Q's?" said Smith, earnestly. "Them's letters, ain't they?"

Mr. Jones agreed.

"Then show us a P, Mister Jones, and then show us a Q, and I'll try to mind 'em!"

For the thought had occurred to Smith that two letters would be a fair start to the day's work of learning to read. Unluckily, Mr. Jones took him for a humorist and aimed a thump that would have been pleasurable if it had struck . . .

"Bleeding scholars!" thought Smith, as he scuttled out of the hangman's office. "Want to keep everything to themselves!"

From Mr. Jones's, it was but a brief (though dark and sullen) way down a ragged stairway, along a passage, a turn to the right, then up two steps, to the Stone Hall where Smith's present hopes were most likely to be passing the time of what was neither night nor day. For the Stone Hall was a long, low, arched room with its own stone sky and its own six lanterns for a sun. When these were lit, it was day: when they were out, it was night . . . no matter what the outside heavens were declaring.

Smith's present hopes shuffled somewhere among the lost multitude of the Town's rubbish and dregs. Grumbling ragbags and tattered felons, debtors who always looked surprised (though God knew why!) and, here and there, like a fallen moon, a pale white face of unbroken pride—most likely of a man due to be hanged.

Here was Smith's place of daily business; for he ran errands for the debtors—twopence a mile dry, and fourpence when it rained.

Very educated gentlemen, the debtors. A man needs to be educated to get into debt. Scholars all. The first Smith tried was a tall, fine-looking gentleman who, though still in leg irons, walked like he owned the jail. (As well he might, for his debts could have bought it entire.)

He smiled. He was never at a loss for a smile . . . which was, perhaps, why he was there. For, when a man can't pay what he owes, a smile is a deal worse than nothing!

"Learn us to read, mister!" said Smith, humbly.

The fine debtor stopped, looked—and sighed.

"Not in ten thousand years, my boy!" he said, and before Smith could ask him why, he told him.

"Be happy that you can't! For what will you get by it? You'll read and fret over disasters that might never touch you. You'll read hurtful letters that might have passed you by. You'll read warrants and summonses, where you might have pleaded ignorance. You'll read of bills overdue and creditors' anger, where you might have ignored it all for another month! Don't learn to read, Smith! Oh! I implore you!"

Then the gentleman drifted, smiling, away, with his back straight, his head held high—and his ankles jingling.

Next, Smith applied to a learned felon, a ferret-faced man with small, starry eyes.

"What d'yer want to read for, Smith? No need. If it weren't for me skill as a reader, I'd not be 'ere today. Was on the run and saw a new goldsmith's sign. Stopped to read it—and 'ere I am! No, stay ignorant, me boy—and keep out of 'arm's way!"

Smith pleaded, but the felon was determined, so Smith left him and would have gone from the Stone Hall had he not seen Mr. Palmer.

This Mr. Palmer was a debtor of a different sort: a gentle, sad man who could not bring himself to believe that the world had been so spiteful as to jail him. (Even though it had been these past five years.) For Mr. Palmer (did the world but know it) nourished a very high opinion of himself, which he was careful to hide for fear of it being damaged.

"Learn us to read, Mister Palmer!"

Mr. Palmer stopped in mid shuffle.

"Learn us to read, Mister Palmer!"

Mr. Palmer turned on Smith a look of amazement that hid a powerful contempt and dislike. Even loathing. For this debtor loathed, hated, and despised every mortal thing that was better off than himself by being free.

"A pleasure to *learn* you, Smith," he said. "Here, boy." He bent down and beckoned. Smith approached. "This is how we begin!"

He seized Smith's nose as hard as he could, and pulled and twisted and wrenched it till Smith's squeals filled the Stone Hall and his eyes fairly gushed with tears! Then his own voice was raised even louder, in a fearful bellow of pain! He'd forgot Smith wore no leg irons—and could use his feet to advantage.

In an instant, Smith had fled, leaving Mr. Palmer with an empty finger and thumb, and a pair of shins that were splintered with booting! He lay on the ground and continued to roar, only braking off to pray that the ungrateful brat who'd crippled him, might come to a bad end on Mr. Jones's rope; while Smith, full of anger and humiliation and a burning pain in his nose, left Newgate Jail swearing a solemn oath that, not till he was took, would he ever set foot in that foul place again!

With his hands pressed to his chest and his eyes still streaming with forced tears, he ran toward the nestling of lanes about the great cathedral. Softhearted ladies stared as he passed, moved by the sight of the weeping urchin. Then his eyes dried up, his nose recovered—and his grand determination flared anew. He *would* learn to read! For he and the document were going up in the world—though the Devil himself stood against them!

Surely the Town had more scholars than those in Newgate Jail? The streets must be full of them! He had only to ask. No harm in asking . . . He crossed the windy street to meet with a round-faced old gentleman with an absent-minded air.

"Mister—mister! Learn me to read!"

The gentleman paused, momentarily taking his hand from his hat. In an instant, the wind whipped it off, together with his wig, leaving him as bald as the dome of St. Paul's. Smith, meaning no offense, began to grin. The gentleman raised his stick—and Smith fled for his life!

He asked a lawyer, a clerk, a country schoolmaster— but they would have none of him. He poked his head through the window of a carriage waiting outside an apothecary's to ask of the elderly lady seated within. But she shrieked and shouted for her footman to frighten him off. At last, he found himself on Holborn Hill, passing by gray, high-shouldered St. Andrew's Church. The Church! Mother of the Town—and all creatures in it!

With renewed hope, he shuffled up to the porch and peered into the richly stained gloom of the church's insides. Blood of glass martyrs fell across the aisle and drenched the altar . . . and there was a smell of damp stone in the quiet air. A very peaceful, genteel sort of place.

At first, it seemed empty, and Smith had some brief thoughts concerning the candlesticks.

"What d'you want, my child?"

A priest was in the pulpit, still as a carved saint.

"Oh it's beautiful!" said Smith, ingratiatingly. "Just like me sisters' stories of 'eaven!"

The priest nodded and smiled kindly.

"What are you looking for, my child?"

"Guidance, your reverence," said Smith, who'd decided, this time, to ask roundabout.

"Are you lost?"

"Oh no, your worship! This is 'olborn 'ill!"

The priest compressed his lips and eyed Smith shrewdly.

Hurriedly, Smith went on, "Learn me to read, your 'oli-
ness! That's what I come for! Learn me to read so's I can
read the 'oly scripture!"

The priest stared in amazement at the filthy, strong-
smelling little creature who stood in the aisle with his
black hands pressed to his grubby heart.

"If you come and stand by the door during Service,
then you'll hear me reading from the Holy Scripture,
child. Won't that be a comfort and help?"

"Oh yes, your grace. And I'm 'umbly obliged. But what
of when I'm 'ome—all in dirt and disorder? Who'll read to
me then? And me two poor sisters: a-panting, a-groaning,
a-supplicating for salvation? Who'll read to them? Oh no,
your reverence. I got to learn to read so's I can comfort
meself in the dark o' the night . . . and light a little lamp in
me sisters' souls with perusings aloud from the Good
Book!"

But this was too much.

"You're a little liar!" exclaimed the priest, abruptly.
Smith gazed thoughtfully up at him, proud in his white
surplice and bands.

"And you're a fat bag of rotting flour!" he snarled suddenly. "I 'opes the weevils gets you!"

So was there no one in all the Town who'd teach Smith
to read?

He passed the top of Godliman Street. A man came out
from somewhere, stopped . . . and stared at him palely.
But Smith, still disheartened by the church's rejection, did
not see him and went wearily on.

The booksellers in St. Paul's Churchyard! A last hope

for the day. And where better to learn to read than in a bookshop?

Several times he idled up and down, judging his chances in each shop. Here, a proprietor scowled at him; there, a clerk shook his fist; and over there an entrance was blocked by a fat man, who seemed to've died in the act of reading, but came to life to turn a page and acknowledge the helpless bookseller with a corpselike nod.

But there was one shop that attracted Smith by the mad profusion and tottery architecture of its wares. Books stood in walls and towers and battlements, as if the owner had been in a state of siege for a hundred years. Which was partly borne out by his appearance. He was an amazingly thin, wary little man with a nervous affliction which made his head dart from side to side as if wondering from where the attack might come. Nor was he put at ease when he saw Smith. For he'd seen Smith before, even knew him . . .

He sat in a curious kind of cave of books where he could jerk and twitch in privacy and quiet.

"Learn us to read, mister!"

"Be off with you!" he said curtly, jerking his head to the right.

"Ain't you got no feelings for yore trade?" asked Smith, earnestly. "Don't you want it to prosper with more readers . . ."

"You're a wicked little thief!" said the bookseller, now jerking to the left.

"Only because I'm ignorant!"

"Get out of here!"

"Why won't you learn me?"

"Keep your thieving hands to yourself!"

"Why won't anybody learn me?"

"Because they've too much sense . . ."

". . . All this goodness and wisdom and learning . . ."
(Smith was grandly pointing to the dusty cliffs that reared
on either side.)

"Touch a book and I'll have you!"

The bookseller was now jerking and twitching pretty
vigorously, and, as his head flew from side to side, Smith
considerately tried to keep pace with it, which made him
appear as if he was performing a frenzied nursery dance.
"Atishoo! Atishoo!"

"Keep still!" shouted the bookseller of a sudden—and
jerked worse than ever.

"We all fall down!"

Smith, capering wider and wider, struck first against
one and then against the other of the two tottering shelves
. . .

The calamity that followed, though of brief duration,
was terrific in its scope. It was as if the long siege was at
last over and the enemy had breached all the walls at
once! For the two walls of shelves had collapsed and with
them, brought down in a mighty and thunderous torrent,
every last item in the whole of the ramshackle shop!

Books in their fluttering and dusty thousands poured
and thumped down as if the very skies had been loaded
with them. Histories, Memoirs, Diaries, Lexicons, Gram-
mars, Atlases, Journals, Biographies, Poems, Plays; books
about Heaven, books about Hell, huge books about
Pygmies, tiny books about Giants—even books about
Books—all, all slid and tumbled into a desperate ruin ov-
erhung by a bitter cloud of dust! And somewhere underneath it all, still jerking and twitching (though feebly,
now), lay the unlucky bookseller himself!

"Gawd!" thought Smith, halfway round the Cathedral

and going like the wind, " 'e must be squashed flatter than an old sixpence!"

But the bookseller was still alive, and, while Smith was still running and wondering hopelessly whom next he could ask to teach him to read, his last victim was being exhumed by neighbors and passers-by. Strangely enough, he seemed almost the better for the disaster, as though all his life he'd expected and dreaded it, and now that it had happened, a load was fallen from his soul. He jerked and twitched hardly at all as he told how it had come about and who'd been chiefly to blame.

"They call him 'Smith,' " he said.

"And where does he come from?"

"Somewhere near the Ditch. I fancy it's the 'Red Lion Tavern' . . ."

The questioner had been a passer-by. The man who'd earlier come from Godliman Street.

A T AROUND five o'clock Smith went home, having spent
every penny he had (except the three shillings he'd
wrung out of Mr. Jones) on meat pie, ale, and tobacco.
And, though there'd been pockets in plenty for the picking,
he'd kept his hands to himself. For the first time he could
remember, he was afraid of being caught: for then he'd
lose whatever might be the benefits of the document which
was still pressed against his chest where it was growing
stained and strong with sweat.

"Hello, Smith! Not nubbed yet?"
Deep in thought, Smith ignored the landlord's pleas-

antry and made for the cellar steps. From below, the tallows gleamed yellow and cast strange shadows on the wall. He began to descend, when . . .

"Stand and deliver!"

A voice like twelve o'clock of St. Paul's roared from the heart of the cellar! Smith started—missed a step, and came down the rest any way but on his feet!

A dangerous, glittering, murdering adventurer of a gentleman in green stood before him, aiming a pistol the scope of a cannon directly at his head! It was his friend, Lord Tom, the high toby, come on a sociable visit.

"Do watch how you go, Smut!" cried Miss Fanny. "Or you'll be coming down them steps stone dead! And *then* where will our dockiment be?"

"Did you see that degrading Mister Jones?" asked Miss Bridget. "For if you didn't, you can go straight out again, broken pate or nothing!"

"Pleased to see you, Lord Tom," said Smith, picking himself up and rubbing his head. "They told me you was nubbed—but I never believed 'em."

"Ah!" said the highwayman, putting up his pistol and smiling sadly through his brackenish beard. "It happens to all of us, sooner or later, Smut. With some, it's sooner: but with Lord Tom, let's hope it'll be vastly the later!"

"And so say all of us!" murmured Miss Fanny, as she might have said, "Amen!"

"Trade been good these past ten days, Lord Tom?" asked Smith, giving over the three shillings to Miss Bridget who hid them somewhere behind the curtain, away from the highwayman's quick green eyes.

"Been on the Finchley Common, Smut, me young friend. Wild and free on the snaffling lay."

"Don't use them coarse expressions," came Miss Bridget's voice. "If you mean pilfering from unarmed travelers, then say so! Or are you ashamed?"

Lord Tom grinned at Smith (who grinned back) and then at Miss Fanny who sighed and blushed.

"Many coaches, Lord Tom? And was there danger?"

"Fine smart equipages, little Smut! Windows fair sparkling with satin and brilliants! Like traveling stars, I tell you! Gleaming in the foggy nights! It's a life, my boy! Stand and deliver! Courteous with the ladies; stern with the gentry. 'Madam, your necklace—if you please! Sir, your purse—or I'll blow your head off!' "

"And did you, Lord Tom?" asked Smith, smiling wistfully at the thought of riding out with his friend . . . which had always been one of his dearest dreams. "Did you blow off any heads this time?"

"Only a pair of coachmen's, Smut! And then unwillingly—they went for their weapons."

"How many coaches did you take?"

"Six, me friend! Six gay glitterers."

"Then where's your profit, you ugly murderer?" came Miss Bridget's voice—for she'd refused to come out and join the company. "Where's the necklaces and purses, sir?"

Lord Tom sighed. "Spent, Miss Bridget, as well you know! That's the way of our lives. Risk all for the chase—then spend the profit in high comtempt. The chase and the danger's all!" (Here, Smith nodded vigorously.) "There was a diamond brooch I parted with for an evening's ale in Highgate, ma'am. And by God, but it was a good exchange! Eat, drink and be merry, as they say—for tomorrow we'll all be nubbed!"

"A pity it wasn't yesterday!" snapped Miss Bridget: and

for the first time the highwayman looked angry. But it passed and he went on with his adventures, to Miss Fanny's admiration and Smith's envy and delight.

"But what's this I hear," he said at length and, with his hands on his hips, his high-booted legs apart, surveyed Smith with an amiable smile. "For the news I hear" (he nodded affectionately to Miss Fanny) "is that *you've* come upon a rare treasure, me lad. Already me rival in accomplishment? Well, indeed—I'm proud of you! A document, I hear tell. And curiously valuable . . . from all accounts!"

"I told Lord Tom," put in Miss Fanny, stopping her sewing with her needle at full stretch. "And we're of an opinion that . . ."

". . . 'tis nothing of value," said Miss Bridget, coming at last through the curtain, her handsome face much flushed. "A property deed, most likely. Of no use to anyone at all!"

"And I say it's a confession, Brid! Reely, Lord Tom, dear, I'm convinced! Indeed, the more I think on it, it had such . . . such a guilty look!"

"Well, then!" exclaimed Lord Tom cheerfully. "Let's put an end to conjecture and see it! Smut, old comrade-in-arms, let's see the document! Lord Tom'll read it for you."

Smith, suddenly uneasy, stared at his two sisters, one frowning and the other softly open-mouthed. Then he looked up to his friend, the glittering, dangerous highwayman. He hesitated . . . and began to back toward the stairs. Now that his secret was about to be revealed, he felt unsure, even unwilling. For a whole day the document had been next to his heart. He felt strangely that he'd be betraying it if he gave it up now. He continued to look suspiciously from one to another of the company.

"Well, Smut, friend—where's the treasure?"

"I—I ain't got it, Lord Tom. I—I left it with a friend."

"Not that creeping saint, Mister Palmer?" exclaimed Miss Bridget. "How I 'ate debtors! They're worse'n thieves."

Smith shook his head and rubbed his nose ruefully.

"Then who's got it, Smut, dear? Who's got our valuable dockiment?"

"The parson in St. Andrew's!"

"And who's 'e, when 'e's at home? You little liar!" said Miss Bridget, coldly.

"A friend o' mine!"

"You made 'im up!"

"No, Miss Bridget! True as I live an' breathe. Big fat man all in white. Friend of mine. Cross me 'eart and 'ope to be nubbed!"

"And where did you meet 'im?"

"In church . . ."

"Now I *know* you're lying, for you never was in a church in all your born days! Liar and blasphemer! Oh how I 'ate a liar! Nothing's more degrading. You come 'ere, you young person, and I'll wash your mouth out with vinegar for you. Don't think you'll escape this time!"

Miss Bridget—who had indeed a jar of vinegar in her hand—began to advance on Smith with her eyes glinting venomously. Smith dodged briefly behind Lord Tom, and hung on to the tops of his boots.

"Never come 'tween a family," chuckled the highwayman—and stepped aside so's Smith stumbled and fell. Miss Bridget came on. Smith howled and fled behind Miss Fanny. Who obliged by crying: "Poor Smut!" and flouncing aside to the stairs.

Smith began to dart round the cellar at so great a rate

that the tallow flames tore after him as if to rip loose from
their seatings.

"I'll teach you to lie to me!" shouted Miss Bridget, making strong dives at her brother, who, between howling and
roaring his innocence, kept dragging table and stools and
every moveable article into her path.

On the stairs—cutting off all retreat—sat Miss Fanny
and Lord Tom, laughing fit to burst.

"Let me through!" panted Smith each time he passed.

"Not till you give up the document," laughed Lord
Tom.

"Oh do as Lord Tom says, dear Smut!" cried Miss
Fanny, "before Brid mashes you stone dead. For she's that
vexed."

Smith shook his head and rushed on more fiercely than
ever: for Miss Bridget, having the longer legs, was gain-
ing. Round and round he scuttled and darted: now like a
sooty moth, now like a quick black rat. And each time he
passed the stairs, he begged and implored Miss Fanny and
Lord Tom to make way for his desperate, panting self.

"Not till we see the document. Ha-ha! Not till you give
up your treasure."

While from behind, Miss Bridget panted grimly: "Nothing'll save you this time! You degrading little liar, you!"

She made a last tremendous lunge—both to save herself
(for she'd tripped on a stool) and to seize her brother's
hair. Smith shrieked. Lord Tom laughed. Miss Fanny
cried: "Poor Smut!" when there was a fateful interruption!
The landlord. His greasy head hung over the stairs like a
dirty street lamp.

"Smith! Smith! Forgot to tell you something!"

Hastily, Miss Bridget let go of his hair and genteelly
wiped her fingers.

"What?"

"You 'ad callers. Two."

"Who? Me?"

"Yes, indeed. Had you off to a 'T': dirty, weaselish, villainous-looking remnant. Eyes like chips of coal. Teeth like the same. About twelve years old. 'That's him!' I says directly. 'Good!' says they. 'And where is he?' 'Nubbed, most likely,' says I. 'Oh,' says they, 'we'll be back, then—to inspect the remains!' Then they was off. No message. Just that."

"W—what was they like?"

"One tall: t'other short. Wearing brown. And, though I says it myself (and I ought to know) as unsavory and throat-slittish a pair as ever I've clapped eyes on! Ha-ha!"

The landlord's head was hoisted out of view and there was a deep silence in the cellar. Smith shivered uncontrollably. He was desperately frightened. God knew how the two men in brown had tracked him down; but they had done so. He could not stop his teeth chattering. Even Miss Bridget looked at him compassionately.

"It—it's them," he whispered. "They've come to slit me throat."

"Don't you worry, me lad!" exclaimed Lord Tom, grimly. "There's no high toby, thief or rascal who'd dare come here when he knows Lord Tom's on your side. By God, Smut! If they so much as sets foot on them stairs, I'll blow blue daylight through the both of them! You've a man to protect you now, and I can't say fairer than that."

"No," muttered Smith. "You don't know 'em. They're not your sort, Lord Tom . . ."

". . . why, Smut! You'll be safe with Lord Tom! There, dear, you just give 'im our dockiment and all will be well."

"You don't understand! They'll do for me anyways.

They're that sort. I seen 'em, I tell you."

"Then what will you do, child?" asked Miss Bridget, much troubled.

"I don't know. But I can't stay 'ere. Not now. Not at night! I'll go off somewhere. Maybe to . . ."

". . . to the parson at St. Andrew's?" smiled Lord Tom.

"Maybe."

"Don't lie now, child. It may be for the last time . . . and you'd go to Hell."

Smith looked round the cellar, which was his home, very mournfully and wretchedly. "I got to go! For Gawd's sake, let me pass!"

Lord Tom shrugged his shoulders, but stood aside. "I'd protect you, Smut. Honest, I would."

"The dockiment, Smut. Won't you leave it dear? It'll bring you no good."

"No!" said Smith, fiercely. "Never! Never! Never!" He paused, as if shocked by his own determination, then added, "besides, it's with the parson at St. Andrew's."

"Oh Smut," sighed Miss Fanny. "Brid's right—and you're a liar! For you got it inside of your coat. I can see it, dear."

"Out o' my way!" shouted Smith—and, with a desperate rush, flew up the stairs and was gone!

TWO MEN—one short, the other tall—who might have
been dressed in brown (the street was too dark to
be sure), saw Smith hurry violently out of the "Red Lion
Tavern." They'd been in a doorway near by. Deep in
shadows. They did not think they'd been observed. After
a few seconds, they set off together in the wake of the
hurrying boy. They followed him for about five minutes
along the nearly empty Saffron Hill. Then they lost him.
He seemed to've vanished into the gloomy air. Half a
minute later, he was seen—unexpectedly—on their left,
at the corner of Cross Street, hurrying like mad. They
nodded—and set off again.

This time, they kept him in sight for nearly ten minutes:

then he vanished near Cony Court. They waited awhile, listening: for the narrow streets and alleys hereabouts were very quiet and even a rat's scuttle would have been heard. Now they entered the shadowy confines of the court; were about three yards within it when the boy was seen again, now darting desperately back toward Cross Street, his alarmed eyes glittering like "chips of coal" in the light of some late merchant's window.

Back went the two followers, their shoulders hunched —for the night was growing bitterer by the minute—and their feet kissing the cobbles with a grim, urgent passion. They did not let him out of their sight for seconds. Portpool Lane—Hatton Garden—Chart Street—back into Saffron Hill, then Holborn Hill—Union Court—Hatton Garden again—and so to Cross Street—Saffron Hill—Cox's Court . . .

An intricate necklace of flight was being threaded as the three hurrying figures shifted through and round the lanes, courts, and alleys that lay, ragged and near deserted, under a gnawed rind of the moon.

Sometimes, there was not above five yards between them, and still they'd lose him for a few seconds—oddly, unaccountably, like he'd gone up in a puff of black smoke —till there he'd be again, come suddenly from some dark passageway of which nothing had been seen till then.

There seemed to be many dozens of these crevices in the black, lumpy substance of the frowning houses but, sooner or later, there'd be one whose end would be sewn up tight as a sock: a fatal passage from which there'd be no panting scuttle of escape . . .

The boy had left the "Red Lion Tavern" at half after six by St. Paul's. At a quarter of nine o'clock, the followers leaned up against a wall in Hatton Garden.

Breathed one: "Fer God's sake, I can't go another step. Me heart'll burst, I swear it!"

Came a low reply, much charged with pain and

phlegm: "All right! We'll go back, some'ow, to the 'Red Lion.' We'll wait there . . . God rot the crafty little perisher!"

With painful steps they limped away—so wind-broken after two-and-a-quarter hours of unceasing pursuit, that they seemed scarce able to drag their own meager shadows down the cold street.

Ten minutes later, in a narrow abutment no more than a yard from where they'd been leaning, a shadow moved. Then a face edged out: a small, pointed, wary face. It surveyed the empty street. It grinned—not with pleasure, but with a savage and desperate triumph. For Smith had done what he'd set out to do when he'd seen the men waiting for him as he'd left the "Red Lion." He'd run his pursuers into the ground!

He began to walk—somewhat slowly, for his own sides were aching villainously. Presently, he stopped and drew the sweat-drenched document from under his coat. He studied it by the thin, cold light of the moon. It did not seem much the worse for its wetting. Miss Bridget's "property" and Miss Fanny's "felonious" looked as much like a horse and cart and a nest of maggots as ever. Nonetheless, at the first opportunity, he picked a passing pocket of a handkerchief and wrapped the document in it. Then he sighed with relief and set off for another part of the Town.

Though no one followed him now, he moved with extraordinary circumspection: for the dark houses and the dimly silvered streets—with their gutters running down their bellies like black wounds—held another, more formidable menace. Time and again, he fancied he heard other footsteps—steps that limped awkwardly—and he thought of the unseen lame man with the soft voice.

But these alarms were in his mind alone, and if they ever came to anything, they never turned into more than the totterings of some drunken homegoer, or the limping of a chairman, weary unto death and cursing under his breath.

Now he was in High Holborn, and the tall buildings on either side scowled blackly down, with, here and there through an ill-drawn drape, a yellow sneer of light; while ceaselessly down the wide street, like the Devil's own crossings-sweeper, came a bitter wind, whipping up the Town's rubbish into spiteful ghosts of dust and paper that plucked and nipped and stung the living boy.

His nose, chin, and fingers were beginning to burn with the cold. Not a night to be out in: black and windy, with the moon now doused in a creeping sea of cloud. He passed by a gloomy alehouse, a bunch of iron grapes groaning from its sign. He stopped, fingered a guinea he'd got with the handkerchief, and thought of a bed for the night.

But the House was full, so he took a half a pint of gin to keep out the cold, the loneliness, and the shifting fear . . . to no purpose. The gin sickened him and inflamed his brain so that he heard everywhere the soft voice he dreaded and the awkward scrape of a leg, quaintly lame. He began to search for the door—and was helped by a pair of potboys who came at him, slantwise, from somewhere in the smoky room.

Out into the bitter street. Above his head the iron grapes creaked menacingly, back and forth . . . back and forth . . . He moved away, fearful that they'd drop and crack him like an egg.

But it was not the grapes alone. The houses seemed to be shuddering against the blotched sky. He shifted out into the middle of the street, for he'd a sudden horror that all the buildings were tottering in upon him. The sky seemed to grow smaller and smaller, and the jagged roofs, fanged with chimneys, seemed to snarl and snap as if to gobble him up.

He began to run, wildly: from one side of the street to the other side, banging into posts, stumbling across the gutter: turning down lanes and alleys that were new even to him . . . And all this with a curious, hopeless urgency, his feet running like a hanged man's feet—seeming to reach for a purchase on a world that was slipping away.

Where was he going? God only knew! Maybe even in search of the two men in brown to give up the document! For suddenly it seemed to him that the document was a fearful disease that was burning and poisoning him—after having tempted him madly from the shelter of his home!

Then was all this frantic flight and fevered imagining the consequence of half a pint of gin? Not entirely. Fears of the malice and rage of stones, bricks, and mortar were a deep part of his nature—which the gin had unlocked. Now a harsh voice seemed to be shouting in his ears:

"The document! Who wants it? Who'll take it? Take the document—and let Smith go home! Here! Here! Here it is, gents! Have it—and for God's sake, let Smith go!"

The voice was his own.

He was in a long, wide street where the moon had widowed all the houses, with black hatchments under their porches. Vaguely, he thought he knew where he was. There was a narrow turning any minute now, an alley-way that would lead him, deviously, back to the "Red Lion." He fancied he saw it. He turned . . .

"Watch out! Watch out! Oh! Oh! Ah!"

At the very moment Smith had turned into the alley, a

gentleman had come out of it. They met: and, though the gentleman was tall and stout and huge beside Smith, he was struck with such speed and force that he fell with an angry, frightened cry. For God's sake, what had hit him? What had rushed out of the implacable night? A murderer? A madman?

Smith struggled to his feet: was about to rush on, when a hand grasped at his ankle!

"Let go!" he shouted.

"Damn you, no! Help me, first."

Smith glared wildly down. He saw the gentleman's face, gray as a puddle; his eyes were sunken and dark. No spark of light in them.

"Help me up! Help me, I say! For pity's sake, sir! Can't you see I'm blind?"

"A blind man," gasped Smith. "Oh Gawd! A mole-in-the-hole!"

The gin's tempest dropped abruptly away, and left a glum wreckage behind . . . bleak and forlorn in the freezing night.

"A boy—a child," thought the blind man, uneasily. "Most likely a young thief. Most likely he'll rob me and run off, frightened out of his miserable wits. Oh God, how am I to get home?"

"If you let go me ankle," muttered Smith, "I'll help you up: that's if you're really blind. Can you see me?"

The gentleman shook his head.

"What am I doing now?" asked Smith, pulling a hideous face.

"I don't know—I don't know! I swear I'm blind! Look at my eyes! Any light in them? Look for my smoked spectacles! They're somewhere about. Look for . . ."

"What am I doing now?" demanded Smith, pulling another, even more monstrous face: for he'd help no one who didn't need it.

The blind man loosened his hold on Smith's ankle and heaved himself up on one elbow. He'd lost his hat and his wig was awry, but otherwise he'd suffered no harm. He began to feel the adjacent cobbles for his possessions. Smith watched him, and his face returned to normal: but, as a last measure, he fished inside his coat and pulled out the document.

"What have I got in me hand?" he asked gruffly.

The blind man sighed. "My life, my boy—my life's in your hand." He smiled wryly. "And—and is that hand as black as the night?"

Smith scowled and put away the document. " 'ere you are, Mister Mole-in-the-hole! 'ere's me black 'and, then. Up with you! Up on yer pins! And 'ere's your hat and stick and black spectacles—though why you wears 'em foxes me! My, but you're a real giant of a gent! Did you know it?" This last as the blind man stood up and fairly towered over the tiny, helpful Smith.

"Thank you, boy. Now, tell me if I'm in the street or the alley and I'll give you a guinea for your pains."

"You're on the corner."

"Facing which way?"

"The Lord knows! I've been sick meself!"

"Fever?"

" 'alf a pint o' gin!"

Suddenly, Smith felt a strong desire to confide in the blind man. After all, it could do no harm . . .

"Smith," he said; and held out one hand to be shook while with the other he guided the blind man's hand to meet it. "Smith: 'unted, 'ounded, 'omeless, and part gin-sodden. Smith. Twelve year old. That's me. Very small, but wiry, as they say. Dark 'aired and lately residing in the 'Red Lion Tavern' off Saffron 'ill. Smith."

Helplessly, the blind man smiled, and his questing hand grasped Smith's—firmly.

"Mansfield," he said. "Blind as a wall for these past twelve years. Well-to-do, but not much enjoying it. Mansfield: residing at Number Seven Vine Street under the care of a daughter (God help her for her sacrifice!). Mansfield: believe it or not—a magistrate!"

"Gawd!" gasped Smith. "Oo'd 'ave thought I'd ever be shaking 'ands with a bleeding Justice?"

If Mr. Mansfield heard, he was too gentlemanly to remark on it. Instead, he fumbled in his coat for the promised guinea.

"And now, just point me toward the church that should stand at one end of the street, and the guinea's yours, Smith, with my deepest thanks."

Smith obliged—and took the guinea.

"Seems a lot for a little," he said.

"Good night, Smith."

"Same to you, Mister Mansfield, J.P."

He watched the blind man tap his way down the street, bumping, here and there, into the posts and sometimes raising his hat to them and mumbling, "Sorry, good sir. Couldn't see you . . . so sorry!"

Smith smiled indulgently: was about to make off, when a strangely familiar feeling of pity stirred in him. He had been reminded of the murdered old gentleman. He scowled at his own indecision, stuck his ancient pipe defiantly in his mouth, and hastened in the blind man's wake.

"That you, Smith?"

Smith grunted.

"Didn't expect you . . . "

". . . going the same way meself."

"To Vine Street?"

"Thereabouts."

"Glad to hear it, Smith."

Smith grunted again: irritably. "Oh well, here's me black 'and, then . . . you old blind Justice, you. Just tell me where to turn and where to cross and I'll see you 'ome safe an' sound. After all, I ain't done much for that guinea!"

Mr. Mansfield found the offered hand and, once more, grasped it. He sighed . . . and, not for the first time, reflected in his heart (which was far from being as blind as his eyes), that it was an uncanny thing to be the cause of kindness in others.

Vine Street lay about twenty minutes away: for Mr. Mansfield had strolled far that night, having a troublesome problem that gnawed him. But now, holding Smith's small, cold hand, the problem sank somewhat.

"Were it a sickness?" asked Smith, after a while.

"My blindness, d'you mean? No. Lost my sight when a house burned down. Lost my wife as well. A costly fire, that!"

"Oh."

"Take the next turning on the left, Smith."

"What's it like—being blind?"

"Dark, Smith. Very dark. What's it like having eyes?"

"The moon's gone in again, so we're two of a kind, Mister Mansfied: you an' me."

The blind magistrate felt somewhat taken down, but was cautious not to show it. Twelve years of his misfortune had taught him that a bland face was the best security for one in his situation . . . and that, for a blind man to frown, scowl or laugh, even, was like a fool discharging

his pistol wildly in the night. The Lord knew who'd be hit
by it.

"If you can see a new-built church with a round tower,
cross in front of it and walk with it to your right."

Smith obliged. Hand in hand, they passed by the church
—a very curious pair indeed: small Smith, half a pace

ahead, and huge, stout Mr. Mansfield, blandly helpless, walking somewhat sideways, behind, for Smith tended to pull, rather.

"Vine Street is the next street that crosses this one. My house is to the right. I'll be safe enough, now, Smith."

"No trouble. I'm going the same way. To the door, Mister Mansfield."

They came to Vine Street.

Said Mr. Mansfield: "If you've nought better to do, will you come in and take a bite of late supper with me, Smith?"

"Don't mind if I do, Mister Mansfield."

"Care to stay the night, Smith?"

"Don't mind if I do, Mister Mansfield."

"Any family, Smith?"

"Sisters. Two of 'em."

"Likely to worry?"

"Not much."

"Then it's settled?"

"Just as you say, Mister Mansfield."

"Anything else I can do for you, Smith?"

Smith sighed ruefully. The only thing he really wanted, Mr. Mansfield was unable to provide.

"No, thank you, Mister Mansfield. You done all you can."

They came toward the door of Number Seven. In spite of himself, Smith grinned at the irony of his situation. Of all the men in the Town to bump into and befriend, he'd lit on the one who was blind and so could never teach him to read!

THOUGH SHE was amiable, charitable, and kind to a degree, Miss Rose Mansfield was not one of your born saints who sing and beam on their bonfires till they're roasted to a turn: potato saints, so to speak. She was made of a commoner humanity than that, and took full advantage of her father's blindness to scowl and grimace—and sometimes shake her small fierce fist—when the blind man's disability caused her irritation or annoyance: which it often did. Thus, when Mr. Mansfield blundered and broke some precious piece of porcelain, she'd cast her eyes to the ceiling—but declare:

" 'Twas only a chipped cup, sir. I promise you, I'm glad it's gone! Come, sir, let me help you."

And her voice was as always: gentle and kind.

For all of twelve years, this outward show of her human feelings, unseen by her father, had somehow created within a disposition of rare excellence, so that, at one and twenty she stood—not very tall but of great consequence —the most kindly, peevish, honest, and remarkable young woman in the length and breadth of Vine Street.

Miss Mansfield stood on the topmost step, full in the light of the porch lamp. Below her waited a footman, ready to help his master.

"Papa!" she cried warmly. "I was so worried! You've been gone so long, sir. I thought you was . . ."

Here she paused as Smith came into the light—and she saw what the blind man could not: viz. that Smith was the filthiest, most wretched, and nearly the most sinister-looking object in the Town. ". . . lost," she finished up, and her face expressed wonderfully her opinion of Smith.

Smith tugged at Mr. Mansfield's hand, for he feared Miss Mansfield would set the footman on to do him a mischief.

"Daughter," said the blind man. "Here's Smith. As good-hearted a child as London can boast of."

Miss Mansfield did not look as though she believed it and answered Smith's furtive, uneasy grin with a strong threat to box his ears. Her face said very clearly, "So! You've deceived him! Very well then! You won't deceive me! *I've* a pair of eyes in my head!" But aloud, she said:

"Pleased to make your acquaintance, Smith. Any friend of my father's is more than welcome!"

"Daughter!" said Mr. Mansfield, mounting the steps and pulling Smith after him. "My young friend's taking supper with us, and then he'll stay the night. For it's very bitter in the air—and he's far from home."

At this, Miss Mansfield looked so little pleased that Smith was amazed that even the blind man wasn't struck by the angry lightnings from her eyes which blazed: "Oh my God! this—this *creature* in the house? And a bed for it? Papa! You go too far! 'Tis too much to be borne!"

"Any friend of yours, sir . . ." she repeated: and bustled back into the house to attend to her father's wish.

They took supper in a back parlor—as clean, spacious, and handsome a room as Smith had ever dreamed of, furnished with mahogany and much neat silver on display. There were pictures on the walls and a fire in the grate—and it was a shame the blind man could see none of it, for a deal of trouble seemed to've been taken.

While they ate, Miss Mansfield came and went some dozen times with amiable inquiries or amusing observations (she was very talkative and spoke rather quick), but always with a look of the sharpest suspicion at Smith, followed by a glance round the room to see what had been stolen. "I know what you're up to!" her angry face said. "But you'll not succeed! Not while *I've* a pair of eyes in my head!"

"A saint," remarked Mr. Mansfield once, when he was assured his daughter was gone from the room.

"Oh," said Smith.

"You don't meet with a saint every day, Smith," said Mr. Mansfield, sounding somewhat offended by the cool response.

"No. You don't."

Just then the saint came in to say Smith's bed was ready in a small room at the top of the house—and to shoot him as venomous and disgusted a look as ever he'd received in his life. He shivered: for he found his haven for the night strange . . . what with the blind Justice and the daughter at odds with herself.

Nonetheless, he was at bottom an affable soul and continued to talk with Mr. Mansfield a while longer. About what? Life in the streets of the Town; life in the "Red Lion's" cellar; life in Newgate Jail; death at Tyburn, and —death in Curtis Court. Yes, indeed, Smith mentioned— almost in passing—the happening that had turned him upside down and inside out.

"Indeed, I heard of it," said the magistrate gravely, "for the gentleman was known and wealthy."

"Poor old so-and-so!" said Smith.

"Did you see him, then?"

"No!" said Smith, quickly: for how could he have known which was the old gentleman unless he'd seen him murdered? And if he'd seen that unlawful act, why hadn't he come forward?

("Smith! You have thereby compounded a felony—and are subject to the selfsame penalty. Death, Smith, death!")

Yes, indeed, Smith knew the law. And he suspected that the magistrate knew it even better.

"No, I never saw 'im. But I 'eard about it. Poor old so-and-so!"

Even as he spoke, some movement in the air—most likely due to their voices—caused the sideboard candles to flicker and jump and glint ironically in the blind man's dark spectacles . . . and cast a shadow upon the opposing wall strangely like the shape of the murdered old gentleman, come quietly into the room to reproach Smith for denying him and to see what was becoming of his document.

"A Mr. Field, of Prickler's Hill, in Hertfordshire. I knew him, Smith. A good, but sad old gentleman. I'd like to have his murderer before me."

"And so would I, Mister Mansfield," muttered Smith, somberly, for he remembered well the old gentleman's look as the knife had gone in. "Why was 'e done in?"

"I don't know, Smith, I don't know. But it's a vile, dark business . . ." Mr. Mansfield's ordinarily bland face grew hard and grim. "It troubles me," he murmured, more to himself than to Smith.

"What troubles you, Mister Mansfield?"

"My blindness. Because I shall never set eyes on that murderer. Because, till the day I die, I'll never know what such a monster looks like. D'you understand me, Smith? D'you understand that, to me, devils and angels are all one?"

Smith did not entirely understand the blind man's eerie sorrow: maybe because his mind was filled with the news that Mr. Field had been wealthy. Hopes of the document were now very high.

"D'you understand me, Smith?"

Smith nodded: then recollected Mr. Mansfield couldn't see him, so he said, "Yes, indeed!" and went on thinking of his prospects.

Soon after this, Miss Mansfield came into the room and declared that it was growing too late to be talking.

"Not so much for you, Papa, but for your young friend. Truly, he looks tired, sir! His bed is ready—and he ought to be in it!"

Which remark, delivered most affably, was accompanied by a casting of eyes to the ceiling which said very plain, "And the sheets he sleeps in will have to be burned! Oh Papa! this is outrageous!"

Smith's room was small and oddly shaped, owing to its

situation under the roof. It was as though the builder, arriving nearly at the summit of his labor, had come upon this extra space by surprise: and, on the spur of the moment, had popped a door and a window to it so's not to embarrass the stairs with leading to nowhere. A bed, a chest, and a chair were the sole furnishings—and a pot of strong sweet herbs. For, though Miss Mansfield could burn the sheets after Smith had slept in them, she could not burn the room: so the herbs were the next best thing.

Now Smith, though he'd slept on straw for all of his life, wasn't so ignorant as not to know a bed when he saw one. He prodded it: he sat on it: he lay on it: he lay in it. He grinned—and directly went to sleep. This had not been his intention. He'd meant to have a great brood on his curious situation and enriched hopes. But the day had been too long for him: and the night too fierce. He was tired almost unto death. He slept without dreaming, without moving. He slept so long and so deep that Miss Mansfield, poking her head round the door in the morning, thought for the instant that he'd perished in the night and left behind him a small, black corpse.

"Smith!" she cried. "Boy! Wake up! Directly!" and she prodded him with a walking stick she seemed to've brought specially for the purpose.

Smith woke up. Saw Miss Mansfield's ferocious concern. Rolled deftly away. But forgot he was sleeping two feet off the floor. Fell. Swore.

"Language!" shrieked Miss Mansfield—and poked at Smith furiously with the stick. He howled.

"What's wrong?" (Mr. Mansfield's voice from below.)

"Nothing Papa! Your young friend fell out of bed, ha-ha! No harm done!"

Smith, unable to reach the door, had bolted under the bed. And there he crouched, very like a mouse, staring at Miss Mansfield's neat ankles and brisk, black shoes.

"Come out!" she muttered, and down flew her head, with her braided hair falling bolt downward to the floor like a pair of handsomely turned table legs. "No one's going to harm you!" And she prodded him with her stick to prove it.

"Are you here, daughter?"

Came a second pair of feet, large and slippered. Miss Mansfield's head—with a last furious scowl—vanished.

"Papa! You shouldn't have come without help! You might have fallen, sir!"

Mr. Mansfield laughed. Miss Mansfield's feet shifted

impatiently. The point of her stick kept prodding her toes—as if in default of another target.

"Morning, Smith! Sleep well? My daughter has a fine breakfast for you! She's a saint, child! As I told you—a real saint!"

Down came the saint's head. "Come out!" said her angry eyes. "Come out, you disgusting object!" Up went her head.

"Mornin', Mister Mansfield." (No quarrel with the blind man.)

"What? Back in bed?" (The slippered feet moved toward him.) "The voice betrays you! Give me your hand—"

Miss Mansfield's head was back again, peering round her father's ankles. Her lips moved. *"Please* come out!" Sourly triumphant, Smith shook his head.

"Where's your hand, Smith?" (Mr. Mansfield:puzzled.)

Miss Mansfield's eyes were filled with tears. "I beg you —for pity's sake, boy!" they implored. "Don't shame me in his blind eyes!"

Bewildered, Smith stared back. The mouse had made a discovery. The cat was as frightened and lost and lonely as he. Which was no comfort at all. Gloomily, he reached out.

" 'ere's me 'and, then . . . you old blind Justice, you!"

Over breakfast, which was taken in the back parlor, Mr. Mansfield said:

"And will you go back to your cellar, Smith?"

Smith shrugged his thin shoulders. Miss Mansfield looked at him—and then to her father in weary aggravation. Did the blind man live but to spite her? What was he thinking of? So why didn't he come out with it, then? Must *everything* be left to her? And so against her better judgment—

"Smith," she said, affecting a careless, everyday tone not reflected in her face. "Mister Mansfield means, will you stay here? And work for your board and keep, of course! For Mister Mansfield is very concerned about you. He thinks you deserve better of the world than you've got. And would give it to you. My father is quite a saint, you know . . . "

"Come, daughter! 'Tis your own idea!"

"Never! Never in ten thousand years! I read it all in your face, sir!"

"My face?"

" 'Tis like an open book to me!"

Smith, his mouth full, looked from one to the other of the Mansfields, each accusing the other of a kindness. He shrugged his shoulders. They might quarrel about it till the end of time. It would make no difference. He wasn't going to stay in that uncanny house. No, sir! Nothing on earth would have kept him with the Mansfields—blind father and mad daughter!

"Then it's settled," said Miss Mansfield, with another irritable look at her father. "Mister Mansfield will employ you in the stables, Smith, and I" (here she looked "God help me!") "will attend to your improvement. For a beginning, Smith, I shall teach you to read!"

Smith stared. Gaped. Poked his finger in his ear and scraped it about. What was it she said? Teach him to read? TO READ! He beamed. And beamed! He couldn't stop himself. He wondered if his face would ever go back again.

"I think he's pleased, Papa," murmured Miss Mansfield in a low voice. "I suppose he's fond of horses."

Mr. Mansfield offered to send a servant to the "Red

Lion" to acquaint Miss Fanny and Miss Bridget with their brother's situation. But Smith said he'd rather go himself. Mr. Mansfield nodded: the lad wanted to boast of his improvement. Smith sighed with relief. The last thing he wanted was his improvement boasted of in the "Red Lion's" cellar! For, though he loved and trusted his sisters, he feared that under such tortures as the two men in brown might inflict, (such as the sight of five shillings—or even four), they'd wag their tongues like a pair of windy flags! "Smut's on Vine Street! Poor little Smut!"

"I'll tell 'em tomorrow," he said: and left it at that.

Now all was settled indeed, and Smith—on Miss Mansfield's orders—returned to his mad-shaped room. In high good humor, he fell upon the bed and took out the precious document—the last remains of Mr. Meadows of Prickler's Hill in Hertfordshire. Excitedly, he waved it aloft like a banner.

"Won't be long now, old fellow! Very soon you and me will be better acquainted! And then—up we'll go in the world!"

Then he folded it and wrapped it once more in the pilfered handkerchief. Not a moment too soon! Footsteps. Quickly, he pushed it into the tumbled bed linen. The door opened. Two footmen with real hangmen's faces. Alarm seized Smith! Why had they come? And why so grim?

"Up with you!" said one.

"And then down with you!" said the other.

"W—what d'you mean?"

They grinned. "Miss's instructions. She says, afore you commence on scrubbing the yard, that selfsame necessary thing must be done to you! So down to the scullery, young Smith!"

Smith's eyes glittered in alarm. Most likely, he paled,

too, but that wasn't so easy to see. He looked about him. No escape. He looked up to the footmen. No mercy: nor even pity.

"To the scullery, young Smith."

Now Smith had never been washed since, most likely, the midwife had obliged twelve darkening years ago. Consequently, he suspected the task would be long, hard, and painful. He was not mistook.

Two more footmen, aproned over their livery, stood ready and waiting by a steaming iron tub.

"Take off them wretched rags, Smith."

"Rags? What rags?" (The scullery was gray and stony and full of strong vapors.)

"Your clothes, Smith. Take off your clothes."

The window was barred and the door was shut. He began to undress. Disdainfully, the footmen watched him: and indignantly, he stared back.

"Ain't you never seen a person take off his clothes before?"

Disdain gave way to amusement—and then to surprise. Several times the footmen reached forward to seize him for they thought he'd finished: but each time he waved them back.

" 'ave the goodness to wait till I'm done, gen'lemen! 'ave the goodness!"

For Smith wore a great many clothes. Indeed, to the best of anyone's knowledge he'd never thrown a single item away, but, when that item had worn almost to nothing, he'd stolen another and laid it on top. Coats and waistcoats worn to nothing but armlets and thread now came off of him, and shirts down to wisps of mournful lace—but one by one, removed carefully and with dignity, then dropped, gossamerlike, to the floor.

Then there were breeches consisting of nothing more than the ghosts of buttonholes; and breeches that came off in greasy strips—like over-cured slices of ham; and breeches underneath that were no more than a memory of worsted, printed on his lean, sharp bottom. These memories of perished clothes were everywhere, but plainest of all on his chest, where there was so exact an imprint of ancient linen that Smith himself was deceived—and made to take off his skin!

At last, he crouched, naked as a charred twig: quivering and twitching as if the air was full of invisible tickling feathers.

"Ready," he said, in a low, uneasy voice: and the four footmen set to work.

Two held him in the tub: one scrubbed and one acted as ladle man. This last task was on account of the water having been dosed with sulphur, and it consisted in spooning off Smith's livestock as they rushed to the surface in a speckled throng.

From beginning to end the washing of Smith took close upon three hours, with the scullery so filled with sulphurous steam that the footmen's misted faces grew red as the copper saucepans that hung like midnight suns on the scullery's streaming walls.

At last, it was done. He was taken out, rinsed, and wrapped in a sheet—the ghost of his former self. For he was now a stark white replica of the previous Smith, and had his sisters seen him, they'd have shrieked and sworn it was his spectral image!

His clothes were burned before his oddly saddened eyes, which eyes were now seen to be somewhat larger and rounder than might have been supposed. But his hair, in spite of shock and scrubbing, remained as black as the river at night.

"Me clothes," he said. "Me belongings. I can't go about like this."

Then he was told a livery was being cut down for him, and he was to go back to his room and wait. He mounted the stairs, much hampered by the sheet he was wrapped in. But there was great determination in him. Even more than ever. Each fresh disaster he endured seemed to strengthen his bond with the document—and whatever it might contain. In a way, it seemed to be payment in advance.

He opened the door to his room. He stared. His eyes filled with tears of horror and dismay. The bed was stripped. The bedding was gone. And with it—the document!

chapter
SEVEN

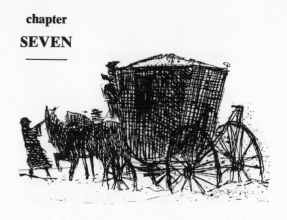

WHEN THEY brought him his fine new livery (blue, with brass buttons), they wondered why he was sat, crouched on his bare bed, with his knees drawn up like battlements before his face. And they remarked, when they left him, on the look in his eyes as he watched them come and go: dismay and despair. They laughed on the way downstairs but not unkindly, and decided his system was still shocked from his washing.

"Give him another half hour and he'll be trying on his new clothes and strutting like the king of the weasels!"

But after half an hour there was no change save that, maybe, Smith's head was sunk a little lower and his eyes stared with a deeper despair. His livery was untouched and the sheet that covered him had slipped an inch or two off his shoulders, leaving those thin objects to fend for themselves against the cold air.

"Maybe he's taken a chill?" suggested the housekeeper and rummaged in her wits for a remedy. "But he ain't flushed or feverish-looking. He looks more froze than inly heated."

Miss Mansfield came to see him. She scowled angrily at his sick, despairing air.

"Are you ill, Smith? What's wrong with you? Answer me!"

"Nothing, Miss. Nothing."

She went away much troubled and ordered blankets to be taken up—and Smith to be wrapped inside of them.

Several times during the afternoon she returned, hoping against hope to find him restored. But each time he seemed more sunk within himself—as if something necessary had perished inside, and all was sinking inward for lack of support. She questioned the four footmen and consulted with the housekeeper—a respectable, stout woman who gave it as her opinion that the child had been poisoned by too much sulphur, and offered to prepare a draught. Gladly, Miss Mansfield agreed. The draught was mixed and carried upstairs.

"Come, Smith. This will make you well again!"

But it was no use. He'd take neither draught nor anything else to sustain him.

"It's as if," said the housekeeper quietly, "that poor mite has made up his mind to die."

"What an idea!"

"Scowl and frown as you please, Miss, but I've seen it happen. These little souls of the Town perish like you and I go to sleep."

And so it began to seem to all the Vine Street household, save Mr. Mansfield himself, from whom it was desperately kept. As was the late visit of a physician—brought in against all dignity through the tradesman's door, with much secrecy and quiet.

He studied Smith. Felt his head, his wrist, his chest. Bade Smith look this way, that way, and to a point above his head. Wearily, Smith obliged: and everywhere his eyes turned they seemed to see even more misery—as if there was no end, no bottom to it. The physician shook his head. In all justice, he could find nothing wrong: but in all compassion and pity, there was something grievously amiss. But it was out of his scope to find it. He spread his hands, pocketed his fee, and left.

More and more, Miss Mansfield blamed herself: for had the child not been bright and well before his violent washing? But to her father's repeated inquiries she answered cheerfully: "He's quite worn out from the footmen's labors, sir. I fancy he'll sleep the clock round. Best not disturb him yet."

During the evening Mr. Billing called. Mr. Billing was a youngish attorney and was both Mr. Mansfield's friend and deeply in love with his daughter. Mr. Mansfield had high hopes of a marriage, but he feared his daughter would never leave Vine Street as long as he lived. For she always laughed when he brought the matter up and declared that Mr. Billing was so agreeable a suitor that it would be a shame to bury him in a husband! Mr. Mansfield would have dearly liked to've seen his daughter's face when she spoke so lightly, if only to see if her eyes were filled with regretful tears. (This was the problem that gnawed him so often—and sent him out into the streets in the night.)

But on this evening Miss Mansfield found the attorney tiresome and overstaying his welcome: for she longed to creep up to the top of the house and see how did the strange, sad child. She had a terrible feeling he'd die in the night.

Mr. Billing stayed and stayed, affable and talkative as ever, and all the while, she longed to cry out: "Begone! Begone! There's a dying boy upstairs, and I must go to him!"

But instead, she helped him to port and brandy (as her father directed), and never left the room for an instant: for she was so guiltily afraid of arousing her father's suspicions that all was not well with Smith. She chattered as amiably as she was able—and hoped her suitor would read the anxious impatience in her eyes. But, unluckily, Mr. Billing was used to Miss Manfield's varied and odd expressions and, though he loved each and all of them, took no particular note of any.

Below stairs, all but two of the servants had gone to bed: a dozing footman and a certain scullery maid called Meg—a softhearted person with large arms the color of boiled lobsters.

For all of the evening her muddled, motherly mind had been fixed on the sick child at the top of the house: and a certain notion had come to her. Knowing that the boy had been brought up in an ale cellar, she supposed he was homesick for all familiar things. She brooded on this till there was no one about to question her, then she crept up to Smith with a pint of ale. Not that she supposed he'd drink it, but she firmly believed that the sight and smell of it would do his aching heart a power of good.

Smith stared up at her mournfully. Her heart was fairly

wrung. She moved about the tiny room to spread the ale's odors. Smith watched her. She smiled—and held out the tankard.

"Come along, little one. It'll do you a power of good. Drink it up, for not the 'Red Lion' itself has a better ale!"

Smith gazed at her somberly.

"Nothing but kindness is meant. All's for your own good! They'll feed an' clothe you an' treat you like a 'uman bein'. You'll want for nought 'ere!"

Smith looked as though all he ever wanted was to pass, unhindered, away. Meg's eyes grew great with tears.

"They 'ad to wash you! You was that black! You should 'ave seen the sheets—"

"The sheets? Did you see 'em?"

For the first time, Smith showed signs of interest in the world. His nose twitched and his eyes began to kindle. ("The ale!" thought Meg, triumphantly. "It's the smell o' the ale what's doing it!")

"Why, bless you, yes! And they was that horrible, Miss wanted 'em burned!"

"And—did you?"

"Lor' no! Burn good sheets? I boiled 'em!"

On this, Smith stared at her so strangely that she began to fidget.

"W-was there anything—anything else w-with the sheets?"

Obligingly, Meg shut her eyes to recall the scene.

"There was a handkerchief . . . but 'twas so far gone I burned it . . ."

". . . BURNED IT?"

Here, Smith gave such a shriek and a groan that Meg thought his last moment was come.

"I 'ad to, little one! 'Twas in a shameful state! It smelled, dear, like—well, I don't know what it smelled like: for I've nought to compare it with! Powerful. Clinging. I only 'ope it'll wear off the master's paper . . ."

". . . paper?" whispered Smith, not daring to hope—and yet not able to prevent it. "What—paper?" His eyes glittered so brilliantly, and he began to shiver so violently, that Meg edged away, fearing a contagious, mortal fever.

"Why—one of the master's documents that had somehow got itself muddled up in that dreadful 'andkerchief. Sometimes he drops 'is papers in the queerest places, what with his disability . . ."

"What was in it?"

"Lor' child! *I* don't know! 'Twas a lawyer's document of sorts—and no one must read *them* save the mistress or the master's clerk. And then only when the master asks!"

"Then how do you know it was a lawyer's document?" (This with desperate sharpness: for Smith was coming back to life with a vengeance!)

Meg, seeing nothing but the boy's improvement and wanting to humor him, smiled confidentially. " 'Twas marked for the attorneys, Billing and Lennard, with 'oom we 'ave dealings." She sighed sentimentally. "Billing and Cooing, I call 'em—on account of Mister Billing being sweet on Miss Mansfield. He's in the parlor now. Such a handsome pair!" Her smile grew soft and misty, then she remembered Smith's question. "So what else *could* it 'ave been but one of the master's documents? Answer me that!"

Dazedly, Smith nodded. What else could it have been but one of the magistrate's documents? For what would a light-fingered scuttle-alley like Smith be doing with a document marked for a lawyer's?

"Did—did you give it to 'im?"

"To our Mister Billing? Lor' no! That's for the master to do! Besides, it were for the other one: for Mister Lennard."

"So you g-gave it to Mister Mansfield?"

"Questions, questions! Was you a cat you'd be stone dead! No: I never gave it to him. There. Why! it smelled so bad it would 'ave knocked him flat—what with 'is disability an' all! I put it in his study along with 'is other papers. Only I put it at the bottom so's the smell might wear off afore he comes to it! That's what makes a good servant," she added, proudly. "Consideration for 'er master's feeling! Oho! there's a good lad! Drunk up your ale! Just 'omesick, weren't you! Knew it all the time! Trust Meg!"

She repeated this several times with some triumph, then beamed encouragingly at Smith and left the room. On the way downstairs she sniffed and tossed her head in high contempt and muttered: "Chills and fevers and sulphury pisonings! 'omesick! Ha! And it took a motherly soul like Meg to see it! Brains? Give you a farthing for 'em!"

She prodded the snoozing footman and boasted of Smith's improvement.

"A touch of 'eart," she said. "That's all this big busy Town 'as need of! Take that boy, f'rinstance . . ." And she described every gathering glint in his eyes: but had quite forgot that he'd gone as white as a boiled shirt when he'd heard Mr. Billing had called.

It was now midnight, and to Miss Mansfield's aggravation and distress, Mr. Billing stayed for another hour. Then at last, he went; and when her father was safely in bed, she flew upstairs with an anguished heart—expecting she knew not what.

She opened the door. She looked inside. She all but dropped her candle! The room was empty! The boy was gone! Her face grew pale with dread. A terrible fear assailed her! The boy, feeling himself to be dying, had struggled from his bed and crept from the house! The housekeeper's grim words echoed in her mind. "These little souls of the Town perish like . . ." So where had he gone? To his wretched cellar? Maybe even now, as she stood trembling in the empty doorway, he was dragging himself through the freezing streets with nothing but the flickering dream of reaching his home? Maybe even now he was dead in some quiet, forgotten court? (With such thorny terrors and poisoned arrows did Miss Mansfield writhe inwardly and suffer her own particular martyrdom.)

In blackest despair she began to go downstairs. Was upon the first floor landing. And stopped. She'd heard a noise. What sort of noise? Very gentle. Very subtle. Very secretive. A papery rustle. Where from? Her father's study.

She approached the door. Her hand was on the handle. She was much frightened. She would have aroused the house, but an odd instinct prevented her. She opened the door. She held up the candle—

"SMITH!"

"Oh my Gawd! I'm done for!"

The floor about Mr. Mansfield's desk looked as though it had been snowed on by documents! Depositions, Confessions, Summonses, and Judgments lay in a guilty profusion: and in the midst of them crouched Smith, wearing only his shirt and looking like an outsize document himself with his face turned up like a gray seal of terror!

All Miss Mansfield's dread and anguish turned now into a violent fury and bitterness.

"*Smith*! Is this how you repay Mister Mansfield? By robbing him? Stealing from a blind man? Is *this* the kindness of heart that so moved him? Nothing but the cunning skill of a cruel rogue?"

She spoke in a trembling whisper, for she dared not awake her father.

Smith, still among the documents, stared up at her with a mixture of misery and fear. He'd not yet found his precious document (which he knew he'd have recognized even among the hundreds he'd strewn about). And now he was done for. Flight was impossible. Miss Mansfield stood in the doorway, and the builder had provided no other way out. He wondered what would be done with him. The worst he could count on was being taken and hanged for a thief. The best—to be sent furiously out into the night. Either way, the document was lost for ever.

"I—I ain't cruel," he mumbled, unhappily. "Reely, I ain't . . ."

Miss Mansfield bit on her lip. She scowled—and her face in the candlelight looked like a small thundercloud. Fiercely, she continued to stare at the unlucky Smith. Really! What could one expect of such a child? All his life a thief! She began to grow angry with her father again. "Sir! You ought to've expected something like this! You're foolishly sentimental, Papa! Just because he showed you a kindness when any other wretch would have robbed you and left you for dead, why should you think he was exceptional? And reformed? A stupid idea, Papa! As if he'd change in an evening! It takes time, sir! And you of all people should have known!"

Her breast began to heave with aggravation: and Smith watched her piteously.

"Papa—you are outrageous! Always you expect me to have the patience of a saint! Well—I haven't! I'm peevish, sir! I tell you: I'm peevish! And now you leave me to deal with this wretched boy while you sleep on in happy ignorance! Oh!"

"Smith," she said, at length, scowling worse than ever under the strain of her long inner quarrel. "I—I'm disappointed, it's true. But—you're fortunate that Mister Mansfield is more understanding than his daughter! *She*, I promise you, would have had you clapped straight into Newgate Jail! But Mister Mansfield never expected an angel out of you all at once. Mister Mansfield's a saint, Smith: and on that account you may thank your stars! Go back to bed this instant—and we'll say no more of tonight. But—but if I catch you doing any such thing again, it's Newgate for you, my lad, on the instant! Now—to bed! Don't gape! Don't cry! Tears won't move me! Or don't you understand, Smith? You've been given another chance!"

T HE HOUSE on Vine Street was both joined to and separated from its neighbor by a brick-built arch that led to the stable and yard. This arch was so clumsy in its brickwork that, skilful as was the coachman, he was forever scraping the paintwork of Miss Mansfield's curricle and her father's coach. But nothing was ever done to remedy this, for Mr. Mansfield had grown used to the sound of it and Miss Mansfield would allow no change to anything that helped her father to see with his ears or hands. So the carriages continued to be scraped and the stableboy was forever being sent to the paint shop for pigment or varnish to make good the damage. Which task fell naturally to Smith. It was on one of these journeys that he fell in with a certain muffin-man with whom he had an old street acquaintance.

"Ain't I seed you before?" asked the muffin-man, puzzled by Smith's cleanliness and livery.

"Maybe," said Smith, cautiously: and then decided to make use of the acquaintance.

"D'you know the 'Red Lion Tavern' on Saffron Hill?"

The muffin-man grinned. He knew it all right.

"And d'you know the two ladies what reside in its nether regions?" (Smith's education had begun and he'd acquired a fanciful taste in words.)

"The darlings in the cellar? Miss Bridget and Miss Fanny? Everyone knows them!"

"The very same! For I'd be obleeged if you'd carry 'em a message."

The muffin-man thrust out his lower lip till it looked like the last quarter of a muffin.

"Tell 'em a—a *certain person's* well and prospering. Tell 'em 'e's on 'is way up in the world—and will communicate further when a suitable occasion has arose."

Much impressed, the muffin-man nodded. "I'll tell 'em."

"Don't forget now. A certain person's on 'is way up in the world."

Then, watched all the way by the admiring muffin-man, Smith strolled back to the house on Vine Street, whistling cheerfully—for he'd just discharged a duty that had been weighing on him these three weeks past. He'd set his sisters' minds at rest (always supposing they'd ever been otherwise), and so had kept his word with Mr. Mansfield. He smiled somewhat wistfully as he pictured Miss Bridget's and Miss Fanny's faces when they would get his news. And he sighed when he thought of his friend, Lord

Tom. Well—well, they weren't gone for ever! Someday, soon, they'd all meet again. When he'd got what he wanted from the document . . .

His face darkened. The document was still in Mr. Mansfield's study, and not all of his wit and deftness brought him any nearer to recovering it. When he was in the house, Miss Mansfield watched him like a brisk and suspicious hawk: and when he was in the yard, the coachman watched him even sharper—while the three ugly, lumbering horses (Smith felt) kept more than an ordinary eye on him.

At night, he dared not try again for Miss Mansfield slept light as a feather—and she'd give him no second chance. His credit on her kindness was stretched to its limit, and he shivered as he thought of its breaking. For he'd come, little by little, to think as well of the Mansfields as anyone else (Lord Tom and his sisters excepted) in the world.

Though both of them, on occasion, frightened him half to death, there were times when they did no such thing. There were times, even, when they made him grin: viz. when they quarreled over which of them was to be blamed for a kindness. There were times when they made him shrug his shoulders in bewilderment: viz. when Miss Mansfield lit candles for her blind father and did everything to persuade the house he could see it. Yet she'd have nothing moved—be it never so awkward and ill-placed—lest her father stumble against it and so betray what the whole world knew: viz. that he was blind as a mole. And there were times when nothing pleased him more than Miss Mansfield's praise of his progress in reading, so that for the moment her good opinion seemed the chief purpose in his studying, and not the document at all! Of which studying, Meg the scullery maid, took a vexatious view.

"Learning?" she'd say contemptuously, while Smith sat in the kitchen of a late afternoon or evening, his small white face cupped in his thin white hands, staring up at Meg's big red face pillowed in her big red arms. "Learning? Give you a farthing for it! Mark my words, little one—a 'uman bein's better off without it! What good's it ever done a soul? Brains? Wouldn't have 'em if you paid me! A penn'orth of heart's worth all your skinny clever heads!" (She stared thoughtfully at Smith's own skinny face and pushed over a piece of pie as if to fill him out as quickly as possible.) "I saw some clever heads—once. When I was a little girl. Me mother—God rest her— showed me. Three of 'em. A Lord, a Sir, and a Mister. On the Traitor's Gate. Cut off at the neck! Very clever heads, they was! And much good it did 'em! 'Meg!' said she—and

I'll always remember her words—'Meg! Take note! Heads without hearts is nought but bleeding pom-poms! Of no use to man, woman, or child!' "

"But at least you can read, Meg," said Smith, munching at the pie. "For you read the name on that old paper you found when I was washed."

Meg stared at him crossly, as if she felt all her warnings were wasted. "I can read what's proper and needful, young man! But no more than that! F'rinstance, I'd never read a *book*!"

"But what about Miss Mansfield?"

Meg shut her eyes in vexation.

"Yes! You look at the mistress! All trouble and worry and storms in the heart! And then you look at the master who can neither read nor write on account of his disability —which is, maybe, a blessing in disguise! All smiles and even-faced! All contentment, *I'd* say! There, now!" (Surprised by her own powers of observation, she opened her eyes triumphantly.) "So, who's the better off? Brains? Give you a farthing for 'em!"

But in spite of Meg's warnings, Smith continued to study as hard as he was able. He mastered the alphabet— that sinister collection of twists and curls and crosses and gibbet-shaped signs that resembled nothing so much as the irons that hung on Newgate's most dreadful walls: and, by the time of his meeting with the muffin-man he could pronounce aloud such words as Miss Mansfield wrote on his slate.

"M-y n-a-m-e is S-m-i-t-h—th," he spluttered out with great difficulty, only understanding the sentiment as he heard the sounds he made.

"Well done!" cried Miss Mansfield: and Smith, though pleased to've pleased her, was mildly aggrieved to discover

that so much effort had gone into saying aloud what was
perfectly well known to both of them all the time. Nonetheless, he was much encouraged, and Miss Mansfield
promised him that, in but a short while more, he'd be able
to read whatever his heart desired. On which Smith's eyes
would stray toward Mr. Mansfield's study with an expression of great yearning and hope . . .

Sometimes, Mr. Mansfield himself would stay to listen
to Smith's lesson: now and then explaining something of
which his poor blind eyes still held the memory. But
mostly he kept silent, save when he, too, had occasion to
praise the boy's quickness and progress. And this, when it
happened, moved Smith oddly: for he sensed a deep generosity behind it, and if anything could bring tears to
Smith's eyes (apart from a thump on the nose), it was the
sudden warmth of a generous heart.

Nor were the Mansfields the only ones who were pleased
by Smith's redemption from black ignorance—which was
following so pat on his redemption from his other blackness. Mr. Billing had come to hear of Miss Mansfield's
pupil, and the lad's arrival and subsequent improvement
at Miss Mansfield's hands formed a fresh subject for his
lively chatter.

This Mr. Billing was a handsome fellow of thirty or
thereabouts. He had rosy cheeks, a prosperous, dark mustache, and eyes that, when they weren't shining with devo-
tion to Miss Mansfield, were shining with all of an attorney's shrewdness and wit. He walked with quick springy
steps and took off his cloak with an air. These facts Smith
had learned from observing him from the dark top of the
stairs for, as Miss Mansfield had never yet seen fit to in-
troduce the stableboy to her suitor, Mr. Billing and Smith
had not yet met; even though he called often and unex-

pectedly, knowing that in courtship the sudden is worth its weight in gold.

Sometimes he'd come midmorning with an, "I was passing and couldn't resist," and sometimes midafternoon with an, "I found myself at your door as if by magic!" Then there'd be much cheerful laughter and in he'd come and settle for an hour, dispensing pleasure to Miss Mansfield and irritation to Smith who was banished to the yard or the kitchen; Miss Mansfield preferred to break off the lesson rather than have her suitor and the stableboy—whose tongue she couldn't answer for—meet face to face.

This uneasiness of hers persisted and even grew, and what at first had been a fleeting and foolish embarrassment became a deep and odd fear so that a meeting she'd begun preventing almost lightly, became an affair of strange importance that must be avoided at all costs.

She'd grown deeply fond of Smith, who'd darted into her heart as neatly as she supposed he'd once darted from doorway to doorway on the freezing, friendless streets. An extraordinary child: a fascinating, quick-witted, dear-faced, obliging, and determined child—but a child whose sometime violent tongue she couldn't answer for, and whose resentment at Mr. Billing's interruptions alarmed her. More and more, she came to dread the meeting she'd so far prevented, but which she knew she could not put off forever.

There's no doubt that by keeping all this to herself she'd helped it grow to formidable dimensions in her mind, but Smith's resentment seemed to be growing likewise—as if his patience was running out. As if there was some goal he'd set his heart on, and the nearer he came to it, the more enraged he was at being delayed.

Which was nothing less than the truth: for Smith was now very close to being able to read. His long battle was nearly won! Letters were making words for him; words were making sentences. Great pages of print that scarce four weeks ago had seemed no more than a mad pattern on the paper, now spoke haltingly to him—even told stories, as if long-dead gentlemen woke up under his struggling eyes, buttonholed his mind, and breathed their thoughts and dreams into it. Gentlemen who were dead and dust a thousand years, stirred and shifted and began to live their lives again.

But still with gaps and lapses and conjunctions of letters that seemed to have no business together. It was these gaps and lapses that made Smith dread that if he recovered the document too soon, it would still keep its secret from him. So he waited for the day when Miss Mansfield should declare, "Smith: now you can read whatever your heart desires."

But with the overattentive attorney's interruptions, that day did not come till a certain Tuesday morning, when the event Miss Mansfield had tried so hard to prevent came to pass, as sooner or later it had to.

"Well, Smith," she said with a proud and affectionate smile, "now all the wisdom of the world is yours for the taking. For you can read, my dear!"

On which Smith's heart leaped almost to the skies; and when there came (as there did at almost the selfsame moment) the familiar double knock on the front door, in place of his customary resentment he felt a grand relief that he could escape to his room and caper and dance in a private triumph.

"It's Mister Billing, miss," he said with a cheerfulness

that amazed Miss Mansfield. "Come a-cooing! So I'll be off and 'ide meself now. The best of luck to you, miss! I'm sure you'll be very 'appy!"

With that, he fled from the library in high delight, and with the best will in the world (for Smith, when he wished anyone happiness, really meant it—happiness being a word he didn't use lightly), stopped in the hall to wish Mr. Billing the same.

"Best of 'appiness in your cooing, Mister Billing!" he cried—then faltered on his way down the stairs.

The rosy-cheeked attorney had gone a deathly white! A look of wild amazement had come upon his face. His eyes had widened; his mouth had dropped open. A shudder went through him. Then, as abruptly as his color had gone, so did he—without so much as a word for the lady of his heart. The door slammed violently and Smith, sensing he was the cause, went hastily to the kitchen, puzzled and vaguely alarmed.

About half an hour after he'd left, Mr. Billing returned —and in a state of such high excitement (said the footman who'd admitted him), that he felt sure the gentleman had at last plucked up his courage to ask for the mistress's hand. He'd been shown into the library where the mistress and master were wondering on his unaccountable departure. The footman had listened for long enough to hear Mr. Billing declare that Miss Mansfield was looking handsomer than ever he could remember.

"So she is," nodded Meg, wisely, "for love paints our faces something beautiful."

Here, the housekeeper—a single lady with a complexion midway between a lemon and a turnip—muttered, "Stuff and nonsense!" but looked very wistful; and Smith, whose uneasiness had taken a sharp turn for the worse on the attorney's return, said, "Thank Gawd!"

The housekeeper looked at him curiously, and Smith, feeling the vague danger past, said, "It was only that I thought 'e'd been took ill before," and went on to relate the brief meeting which he'd previously kept to himself.

The coachman, who'd come into the kitchen for his morning mug of ale, shook his head with all the pessimism of a man whose days are spent reasoning with horses.

"Mark my words, he's most likely got a wife and child in Clapham or somewheres an' the sight of our young Smith reminded him! Small wonder he went white. Any man would."

"Stuff and nonsense!" declared the housekeeper, looking even more wistful. "Nothing but biliousness. There's a deal of it about. Just popped out to clear his head. Very sensible."

But Meg was of the opinion that Mr. Billing's sudden pallor and departure were due to nothing other than a brief loss of courage in his heart's intentions which he'd forthwith gone out to strengthen at the nearest tavern.

"I'll wager he'd a smell of brandy about him," she said.

These three opinions now provoked the Vine Street household into a lively dispute for some minutes, during which the coachman's was rejected with contempt, and the housekeeper's thought the most likely. But it was Meg's that won the day, for the Vine Street household was of a sentimental and hopeful turn of mind and always looked forward to the time when Miss Mansfield's tempestuous person should be removed, happily, to another establishment.

The footman who'd answered the door now agreed that

there *had* been a brandyish air about the attorney, and a parlormaid who'd been listening at the library door, came down with the news that the attorney seemed tongue-tied —a sure sign, for someone in his calling, of being in the last extreme of love.

On this, there was a general burst of smiling and pleasure, and the unfortunate coachman had his elbow jogged as he sought to hide his pessimistic face in his mug of ale. Then Meg, in a mood of powerful tenderness, laid her large arm about Smith's shoulders and declared:

"And this little mite's the one who's brought it all on! For the mistress has grown that tender since he's been with us! He's warmed her heart and opened it up to Mr. Billing's cooing. It would never have come about without our little Smith. So give honor and kindness where the same are due!"

With that, she imprinted a large, moist kiss on Smith's surprised face. He blushed—and everyone laughed, including the coachman who laughed loudest of all. So in a matter of moments Smith was become quite a hero, and when the parlormaid (who'd gone back to her post at the library door) came down with the news that Smith was wanted, everyone—even Smith himself—was convinced it was because Miss Mansfield wanted to show off the wonders she'd worked in him. He got off his chair and straightened his coat. The housekeeper found a comb and brought order to his hair. A footman wiped a smut off his face; another suggested a quick bath—and chuckled.

"Go on up, Smith! Do us all proud, Smith! God bless you, Smith! Don't forget, Smith: we're all behind you, lad!"

And so they were for, as Smith went proudly up the stairs, the Vine Street household followed closely after to give him a last pat on the back as he knocked on the library door and went inside . . .

It was just on midday. A brisk fire was burning in the library for the weather was turned very bitter and the sky bulged with unshed snow. For a second time Smith and Mr. Billing stared at one another: and for a second time the attorney shuddered—to the depths of his soul, it seemed.

"It is him. This is the boy I saw. In the Court. This boy stabbed Field. I saw him! He is the murderer! My poor friends—how monstrously you've been deceived!"

For Mr. Billing was the man from Godliman Street: the same man who'd questioned the unlucky bookseller.

GREAT HOPES, great joy, great trust, when they fall do so swiftly—in a bleak and evil instant. They do not diminish little by little, so that a man you trusted yesterday, today you trust a little less. He is lost, damned; nothing of him remains but what is false as quicksand, or . . .

"Snake! Venomous little snake!"

From outside of the library door where the Vine Street household was gathered, eager and close, to hear its prodigy's triumph, came this single, bitter, trembling voice.

"Snake!"

Whether it was the housekeeper's, a footman's, the coachman's—no one knew. It was of no consequence. It

was the voice of the household, shaken and shocked out of
its pleasant dream by the dreadful words of the attorney!

Within the library the brisk fire still danced and
gleamed on the polished wood, the calm brown walls, and
the gilded backs of the books . . . but to Smith, it was
suddenly the fire of Hell.

Miss Mansfield—elegant, handsome, and gay in a yellow brocaded dress—had lost every scrap of her complexion. She'd put her hand to her face as if to hide her horror
and dismay from the world. But her wild dark eyes betrayed her, however much she might cry out:

"No! No! It's not so! You're mistook, sir! Not this boy!
It cannot be! A horrible, horrible mistake!"

For in her heart of hearts, she believed the attorney.
Not because she wanted to, but because she dreaded to!
Because Smith had come to mean so much to her, she
painfully endured his being sacrificed.

"No! No!"

"It is the boy I saw from my window in Curtis Court. I
saw him struggle. I saw him stab. I saw him escape. There
is no doubt. I wish to God there was. Forgive me."

The attorney spoke low and shakily: but his eyes were
cold as stone. If anything gleamed or flickered in them, the
terrified Smith never saw it. If anything pricked in that
subtle, black, and dreadful place that he suddenly and
fearfully divined was the attorney's heart, there was nothing to show for it. Save once. When Miss Mansfield cried
out for a second time. There was in her voice such a world
of misery that Mr. Billing's white hands clenched and he
seemed to flinch—as if his real love for Miss Mansfield
had moaned: "You're murdering me, Thomas Billing!"

Miss Mansfield moved, and the rustling of her dress was
as a dragging sigh. She crossed the room to her father—

that motionless man in his high-backed chair. She made to lay her hand on his (which was fixed upon his stick), but he sensed her intention and waved her off. The customary blandness of his face seemed carved out of granite.

While Smith—Smith, who'd done nothing—*could* do nothing but moan in a dreadful amazement several times over, "You're mad! You're mad! I never laid a finger on the old man! I never touched the old man! I never—never —never . . ." He retreated from them and began to glare very hopelessly about the room: to the Mansfields, to the window (against which stood the sorrowful, terrible attorney), to the door (behind which was the Vine Street household).

No way out. Thoughts—such as they were—whirled in his head and made him feel sick. The blow that had fallen was inexplicable, frightful, crushing. He crept to Mr. Billing. Stared up at him very piteously.

"You—you was wrong, Mister Billing! For Gawd's sake, tell 'em! For you're a-killing me!"

But the attorney shook his handsome head.

"Not wrong, Smith. I saw. I know."

"Then damn you!" shouted Smith—and flew to the Mansfields: blind father and tragic daughter.

"Miss! You knows me! I never done it! Swear on the Scriptures! Swear! Swear! You believe me, Miss Mansfield? *Please* . . ."

In an inward agony Miss Mansfield stared down at Smith, and then to the sad, but certain attorney—who seemed to have no reason in the world to lie. Maybe she remembered the Smith who'd first come to her—and tried to rob her blind father's study? Maybe she thought the boy's fall was a punishment for her own heart and pride in imagining she'd redeemed him? Who can tell what went on in her unhappy soul!

"Oh Smith!" she whispered: and turned away!

"Then damn you, too, you Bedlam-mad saint!" wept Smith, helplessly, and bent down, crouching, at the magistrate's feet: his old blind justice, his mole-in-the-hole.

"Mister Mansfield! *You* believe me! I know it! I can see it in your—your . . . You know me—and I know you! You know I never done 'im in!"

But the magistrate—to whom justice was the only fixed thing in a dark, uncertain world—said nothing. He was casting out of his heart and mind everything save the attorney's measured words and the urchin's frantic denials. Word against word.

"Mister Mansfield!" whispered Smith, staring up and seeing his own face distortingly reflected in the blind man's black spectacles. "You *must* believe! It wasn't me! It was them two men in brown and—"

"—two men in brown?"

"Yes! Yes! And—"

"—you saw them kill him?"

"I—I—"

"Yet—you told me once you'd never seen Mister Field!"

Too late Smith realized he'd ruined himself! Now he was done for . . .

The blind man sighed like the winter wind.

"So . . . so . . . it was you who killed him."

The world fell away and Smith, still crouching on the floor and watching the blind man's lips, felt as lonely, bitter, and forlorn as if he was already on the gallows. Softly, the blind man went on:

"Which hand did you use, Smith? Was it the one you gave me that night we met? Was it that same, small, helping hand? Tell me, Smith! Don't be ashamed—for didn't I say to you that devils and angels are all one to me? Come, little murderer! Was it that hand?"

"Voices in the night!" muttered Smith, despairingly. "We're all voices in the night to you—you poor old blind fool!"

"You will be committed to prison to await your trial."

"Trial? What d'you want to try me for? Might as well do me in now. What's one voice less in your noisy night, Mister Magistrate Mansfield? You'll never see me face when I'm nubbed. Nothing'll 'aunt you! You done right, you have! All I 'ope is—fer your sake and mine—that if you goes to Heaven, then I goes to Hell! For I wouldn't want you to clap even dead eyes on me!"

"Smith—"

"I never done it, Mister Mansfield."

"You'll be tried—"

"—and nubbed!"

"God have mercy on your soul!"

"Not if He's a blind old gent like you!"

"Smith—"

But Smith did not say another word. He shook his head with an air of grimness and despair. He had retired a great way within himself, and whatever he found there seemed to absorb him entirely.

He was much mishandled as he was bundled into the coach for the Vine Street household were very bitter and outraged by the monstrousness of Smith. Even those who —but an hour before—had decided once and for all that there was much goodness in him and had vowed never again to judge by appearances, even they thrust bleak and savage faces close to his, to let him know what the world now thought.

There was a good deal of treading on his feet and jerking of his clothes. Two of his bright buttons were torn off and the side of his face was bruised. But all he did was to shake his head endlessly . . . even to the one kindly face that managed to push its way in among all the anger and contempt to look at him through the coach window. It was Meg, the scullery maid. Her eyes were as large and round and wet as Margate oysters.

"I'll come and see you, dear! I'll bring you something nourishing! Don't fret, little Smith! Meg won't forget you, dear!"

In the general commotion something had been forgot: or would have been but for the scrupulous attorney.

"Wait! Wait!" he shouted from the window. "The warrant!"

The warrant was sworn and witnessed.

"I'll take it down, sir."

The magistrate nodded, wearily.

"And I'll go with him to the Jail."

"There's no need, Billing. There's no need for you to endure any more."

"I'll go, sir. It—it's the least I can do. Let the wretched child have some company on—on his journey. I'll see him decently lodged."

Miss Mansfield raised her eyes to Mr. Billing. Their look much moved him.

"We thank you, sir—for this—kindness." She sighed. "I blame myself for this. It was I who encouraged the boy.

My father was not a party to it. But he was too kind to urge his better judgment. And now—and now . . ." She spread out her hands and shook her head. Then she seemed to recover herself somewhat, and frowned in a semblance of her old manner. "Papa! You have a donkey for a daughter! A sentimental foolish donkey! So we must be thankful for Mr. Billing who's proved himself the best and truest of friends!" She curtsied. "Your servant, sir. Your very humble servant!"

The coach was waiting, much scraped from a more than ordinary collision with the uneven arch. Within crouched Smith, wiping his face from where the coachman had spat in it.

"To Newgate!" ordered the attorney: and joined his victim.

The coach moved off, and for a little way the two occupants stared at each other: the one, incredulously—the other, calmly. Then, when the wheels had settled down to a steady, loud rattle, Mr. Billing leaned forward.

The skin round his eyes puckered somewhat, as if to suggest a smile. But his eyes were still like stone.

"Give it to me, boy."

Dully, Smith began to comprehend. He stared back at the attorney with violent hatred.

"For God's sake, boy! There's not much time! Give it to me—the paper you stole from the old man! Let me have it—and you can go!"

"I ain't got it."

"And I know you have!"

"Search me—or are you afraid of being bit? For I'm a wenomous little snake, I am!"

The attorney looked at the boy sharply: then withdrew

the hand he'd held out. He shook his head with a curious air of gentleness.

"All right, lad, I believe you. What was in it?"

"Don't know."

"Then—where is it?"

"Don't know."

"Doesn't your life mean a fig to you?"

"Don't know."

Mr. Billing compressed his lips, then shook his head again with the same strange gentleness as before. He sighed.

"You're foolish, young man! I promise I'll help you: but you must tell me. It's your only chance. All right—all right! Keep silent now, if you must. I'll understand. But believe me, young Smith, I'm your truest friend! And soon you'll come to see it. Not today, nor even tonight—but tomorrow, maybe. I'll visit you, boy—and we'll talk again. Lay our cards on the table, eh? And then—and then, who knows but we may be friends? You and me, Smith. Don't look so despairing, son! I'm not a villain! It's this vile world we live in, boy!"

But Smith continued to look despairing, for he was much confused by the abovementioned vileness . . . and the blow that had befallen him was more terrible even than the attorney guessed at.

The document was lost: and though at last he could have read it, it was further away from him now than ever it had been since he'd picked Mister Field's pocket. It had brought him nothing but disaster. But it seemed his life depended on it. He hated it: he dreaded it: yet it was as though he'd sold his soul for it . . .

"Newgate Jail, sir!" shouted the coachman, grimly.

Mr. Billing sighed—and Smith groaned . . . while the

birds on Old Bailey and St. Paul's screeched out in high triumph:

"Jug him! Jug-jug-jug him!"

For at last, they were about to be obliged.

THERE LAY in Newgate a very famous felon whose days were drawing to a close. Indeed, on this Wednesday there was less than a fortnight's life in him: for on Tuesday, January twenty-third, Dick Mulrone was to be taken out and hanged. A great many petitions had been got up to save him, but none had succeeded: and no one in his heart of hearts was truly sorry, for the death of a hero (even though he was a murderous ruffian) was a vastly romantic thing.

From morning to night there was a press of carriages outside the jail for Mr. Mulrone had more friends and admirers than he knew what to do with. They came to see him, to talk with him—even to drink with him—and then go away and brood on the frailty of human life (Mr. Mulrone's, not their own).

Even great ladies came and went, their huge skirts swinging and pealing down the doleful passages like so many brocaded bells, tolling: "What a pity! What a shame! Dick's to die on Tuesday week! What a pity! What a shame! Poor Mister Mulrone!"

So it was that Smith, and his bitterness and bewilderment with all the world, dropped into Newgate with no more stir than a driblet of spittle into the Fleet Ditch. True, the jailer at the lodge had been surprised when he'd discovered that the undersized object in livery was Smith.

"Not old Smith?" he'd said, with a shrug and a grin. "Not grubby little Smith? Thieving Smith, Smith o' the doorways and corners? Smith o' the stinking 'Red Lion'?"

Then he'd thrust his reeking, bristly face close and remarked on Smith's cleanliness and said he'd never suspected his features were so human.

"But washing ain't exackly been profitable, eh? For yore dirt, Smith, hid a multitude o' sins, and now them sins is exposed to the view. So here you are, me lad: jailed, jugged, and bottled—as we say in the trade!"

But when he learned the charge was murder, he withdrew somewhat and said reproachfully:

"Ah now, Smith, that's bad! Poor Miss Fanny and Miss Bridget! When they comes to alter them clothes—why! they'll wash 'em with their tears!"

Then Smith was lodged in the Stone Hall, but was spared fetters on account of Mr. Billing's having paid the jailer the necessary dues. Which charitable act had been accompanied by a whispered, "Don't take it too hard, lad!" and a look as deep as the ocean. Then Stone Hall was locked and Smith was, for the first time, a resident in it and not a visitor. A dark and lonely time for him . . .

Though he'd been shut in Stone Hall as a kindness—there being worse places in the jail where he might fairly have been lodged—he dreaded meeting with old acquaintances now his circumstances were so come down. He shrank from Mr. Palmer and his friends for he remembered, burningly, that he'd last parted from them with some defiance, being on his way up in the world. But mercifully, he was spared Mr. Palmer's sneers and scorn. The gentleman was otherwise engaged. Indeed, all the superior debtors were, at that time, too full of Dick Mulrone's grand visitors (and lived in the unlikely hope of exciting genteel interest in the sadness of a fallen gentleman's lot) to spare a glance for the dismal, fearful, pallid child who crept from corner to corner like a persecuted ghost.

The only soul to pay him any heed had been an old man who'd not seen daylight for fifteen years. This queer old fettered bird slept in the fireplace all the year round, save on Christmas Day when the fire was lit (when with much good-natured laughter they shoveled him out), and had come to resemble a dusty ember.

He beckoned Smith over with four or five sharp gestures, and offered to share his strange nest. Salubrious, he said it was, owing to a good down draft from the chimney. With a clank of his fetters he pointed upward to the ragged black hole and declared (though it was impossible), that sometimes a star might be seen, twinkling away like it was sat on Newgate's roof.

"It ain't so bad, little sparrow! You gets used to it. Though we never sees the sun, we never gets doused by the rain, neither! And it's a comfort to know you're in the worst place in the world—so you've nought more to fret and worrit and slave about to keep yourself from falling lower. For you've arrived!"

Then he settled back on his haunches and appeared to doze off, leaving Smith to stare up into the darkness where he seemed to see Mr. Billing's ocean-deep look. From time to time, the old man—now sunk into a nesting coil— would twitch and jerk in a curious fashion, bringing his chained wrists together and thumping them down as if on a hated head. This done, he'd sigh and settle down once more into a contented sleep—till the next time.

Smith shivered—and wondered if the old man, too, had his Mr. Billing and Mansfields to plague his very sleep. For Smith had come to hate the Mansfields more, even, than he hated Mr. Billing. Once he'd admired and even loved them. He'd respected them—and trusted them. He had, so to speak, made great exports from his heart toward them: and had reasonably expected some sort of return. But at the first squall they'd defaulted—bankrupted Smith, and left him in a state of blind and bloody rebellion. If ever Mr. Billing was to get him out of the jail, Smith would make it his business to take a good revenge on the saints of Vine Street.

This resolution, in part, calmed him, though the mystery that clung about Mr. Billing, the document, and— worst of all—the unseen man with the limp (the memory of whom still chilled Smith's blood uncannily), remained as dark and menacing as ever. He fell asleep and dreamed he was being strangled by an enormous snake . . .

Next day, at about ten o'clock in the morning, Smith had visitors: Miss Bridget and Miss Fanny. He was both pleased and surprised. How had they learned so soon? Miss Bridget sighed bitterly and remarked that bad news travels quick: for while it took three weeks to learn that

Smith was going up in the world, it took but the same number of hours to discover he was come down.

"And a common jailer has to tell us! Oh, the shame of it! The degradation!"

Dismally, Smith picked at his brass buttons and neat coat as if to show he wasn't altogether beneath contempt.

"Fine clothes and a clean face are but the trappings of shame," went on Miss Bridget, with furious sorrow, "when the child what has them is so degradingly jugged! Oh!"

"I never done it!" said Smith. "You know I never done it!"

"You're here, ain't you?" said Miss Bridget, unhappily. "That speaks volumes, don't it? You done something!"

"I was wrongly accused! Wictimized!"

Said Miss Fanny: "Innocence is no excuse in the eyes of the Law, Smut, dear. *That* much even your sisters know!"

They stared at him angrily and tragically, while he looked back with as much of defiance as he could manage. Then Miss Fanny, as was her nature, thought of a brighter side. She sighed and poked at her grandiose hat. (When the sisters went out of their cellar they always dressed in the height of every imaginable fashion by way of advertisement.)

"But leastways, 'tis lucky you picked on such a time to get nabbed, sweet. For with dear Dick Mulrone in residence, the tone goes up, don't it! My! but there's fashion and elegance coming and going! Don't you think, Brid, 'twill do our Smut good to be mixing with such gentility? As I always said, 'tis an ill wind that don't blow the silver lining out of the dreariest cloud!"

She sipped genteelly at her gin (they were in the taproom), and made a face. Miss Bridget, who was drinking ale, put down her pot and looked at her sister scornfully.

"Much good his gentility will do him when that disgusting Mister Jones has done with him! It's his clothes that'll be coming down our steps with no boy inside of them, Fanny. And have you thought, sister, what it'll cost to have possession of him for to bury him proper and decent? Or would you have him be took off to Surgeon's Hall to be bottled for all the world to jeer at?"

Miss Fanny shivered and shook her head: then murmured, "Oh Smut, dear, if only you'd given up the dockiment when Lord Tom asked, then there'd be no Surgeon's Hall, nor Mister Jones—nor even them two fierce gents in brown—"

"—did they come back, then?" muttered Smith, coming out of his pint pot of ale, where he'd been hiding his face while his sisters disposed of his remains.

Yes, they'd come back—and back again. They'd haunted the "Red Lion" for several days. A terrible pair with eyes like burning coals; though the taller of them (said Miss Fanny) might have been more presentable if he'd been on the snaffling lay instead of on the sneaking, throat-slitting budge.

Here, Miss Bridget remarked that Miss Fanny's language was as bad as her low-class friend's. To which Miss Fanny said gently that she liked to find good in everyone; and that, had it not been for dear Lord Tom, the villains in brown might still have been there.

"For he took them on one side, Smut, and spoke to them so fierce that they've never been back since that moment! Which, as it turned out, was the selfsame day as that good-looking muffin-man called and said 'a certain person's on his way up in the world,' and told us where you was."

Then Miss Fanny went off into a melancholy memory of how cheered they'd been to get the good news. Which had the effect of disheartening Smith into miserable tears —while round about them the bitterest dregs of the Town ebbed and shuffled and flowed in ever-changing groups and pairs, sometimes eyeing Smith and his visitors with sneering curiosity, but more often discussing the latest news of doomed Mulrone.

Smith's fireplace companion alone seemed to keep his interest: he crouched but two yards off, with his head on one side and his old, bleary eyes quite sharp—like an ancient parrot's. Contrary to her usual habit, Miss Fanny saw no good in him at all, but shuddered to the depths of her soul whenever his old, old eyes caught hers.

Then at last, to Smith's great pleasure and pride, Lord Tom joined them. He'd come from paying his respects to his old comrade-in-arms, Dick Mulrone. He wore a melancholy, romantic air like a new green cloak, and seemed to swirl it from the tips of his ragged eyelashes to the ends of his powder-stained fingers.

"Well, Smut me lad! Alas! it seems you've forestalled me! Not lost, but gone before, eh?" He sighed. "Oh me boy! You go in good company! The best i' the world! For, though I'm a Finchley Common man and poor Dick's a Hounslow Heath boy, I give him best! The grandest of the roisterers! The gayest, dashingest, noblest of us all! He's in good spirits, lad! Ha-ha! The best—for he's drunk as a lord!"

"Disgusting!" muttered Miss Bridget, and drew her discreet finery as close to her person as her hoops allowed. Lord Tom sat back with a toby-sized sigh and his glittering eyes roamed the horrible, stinking, shadowy, shuffling room—maybe with a touch of compassion—or was it only dread?

Smith looked very piteously from his sisters to his grand friend, and the world seemed—even in the Stone Hall—too fair a place to be leaving after so few years in it. Suddenly, Lord Tom's eyes flickered as if some distant shade had provoked a thought. He bent forward to his small friend.

"But we'll see, me fine lad! Yes, we'll see! While there's life, there's hope—as we say on the lay! Maybe Mister Jones won't have you yet awhile? Maybe Lord Tom can help?"

Smith, though not convinced, was sensible of Lord Tom's aim to be cheerful. He looked up with a mournful smile.

"How, Lord Tom?"

"That document, young fellow! D'you have it still?"

"N-not with me, Lord Tom."

The highwayman looked doubtful—then brightened again.

"But d'you know where it lies?"

"That I do, Lord Tom!"

"And, given certain circumstances—such as you might know best—could you lay your hands on the aforementioned property?"

"That I could, Lord Tom!"

"And would you, me boy?"

"That I would, Lord Tom! With all me heart!"

"Then we'll see, me bright young heart! Dark though these matters be, while Lord Tom's about there's yet a ray of light!"

A noise like water running down a choked kennel

denoted that the fettered old man had found some cause for laughter. Then, either offended by the old man's mirth, or from some deeper cause, Lord Tom spread out his strong arms to escort Miss Fanny and Miss Bridget away. One arm was took, but the other was left like an empty bracket: Miss Bridget had no need of support. She fidgeted with her hands, and then, with a strange timidity, stretched out and fleetingly touched Smith's sunk head.

"Be back tomorrow, you—you felonious child! Just remember—though you be—not so good as you ought—you ain't forgot, dear. Fan and me'll be back!"

When Smith raised his head they were gone: but on the table beside his empty pot was a guinea. Which one had left it? Smith scratched his head—and looked to the old man who seemed to've gone off into a dozy brood. The old man yawned, flickered his eyes—and divined Smith's question.

"Ah, me sparrow! That would be telling, wouldn't it! Which one cares a guinea's worth? The pigeon? The starling? Or that seedy hawk? He-he! It's worse than not knowing who's done you an injury—not knowing who's done you a kindness! It's horrible, not knowing who to thank!"

But before Smith could abuse the old man, another visitor came quickly toward him. He and Smith's earlier visitors must have crossed paths without knowing it. It was Mr. Billing.

He saw the guinea and nodded as if it was a portion of an estate he was administering—and accounted for. He wore black, which gave his complexion an oddly high, artificial air. The old man looked at him uneasily, and then clanked further off—as if anticipating the attorney's wish. He turned his bony back and seemed to absorb himself in a corner.

"Well, lad," murmured Mr. Billing, sitting down and fingering the guinea idly, "as you see, I've not forgot you."

"No, Mister Billing," muttered Smith, watching his money being scratched at by a neatly polished claw, "I don't suppose you 'ave. And I've not forgot you, Mister-lying-Billing—Mister-murdering-Billing. Not till Mister Jones turns me off up the road will I forget you! And if there's sich a thing as ghosts, Mister-conniving-Billing, there'll be a screaming, shrieking ghost awaiting you for every night of your life when you goes to bed!"

The attorney looked momentarily taken aback by the force of Smith's bitterness and gloomy hate. Was it possible he hadn't expected it?

"I—I'm not a bad lot, y'know. I live in the world, so to speak, and can't help being of it. Take me all in all, I'm no worse than anyone else. Believe me, young man, you'll come to see that! Life's a race for rats, and it's Devil take the hindmost, the foremost, *and* the one in the middle! We're all rats, Smith—and it's eat or be eaten! Blame Nature, if you like, but don't blame me!"

Having delivered himself of this, Mr. Billing contrived to look oddly wistful—as if he wished the world was constituted otherwise and he might then be as honorable a man as could be met with in a month of Sundays.

Smith looked up at him dubiously, but couldn't help observing that, no matter what melancholy sincerity there was in the attorney's face, his fingers continued to play with the guinea like a cat with a fledgling bird.

"All right, then!" sighed Mr. Billing at length, administering a final tap to the coin and blinking his stony eyes. "Don't trust me. I don't blame you. No! If I was in your situation, I suppose I'd be just as suspicious. Good God! It's human nature! But I'll tell you here and now, my friend (and I *do* think of you as my friend, Smith . . . I like you, you know!), I'll have you know I've saved your life!"

"By having me nubbed?" asked Smith, much bewildered by the talkative attorney. Mr. Billing smiled playfully, and shook his head.

"They knew you were on Vine Street, Smith."

"Who did?"

"The two men in brown. And they'd have come to murder you if I'd done nothing and left you there."

"Ain't they yore friends, then, Mister Billing?"

The attorney looked about him quickly, then bent forward so's his red lips were close to Smith's dusty ear and his sharp mustache pricked and scraped almost painfully.

"Listen, friend!" he whispered. "I'll lay my cards on the table! Open and above board! I'll not lie to you for I like you. We're two of a kind, Smith, you and me. Men who know what's what in the world. Eyes open, chins up—and outface the Devil!"

Despite himself, Smith felt flattered for he was but twelve and small, while Mr. Billing was a grown man. He began to think less harshly of Mr. Billing. A rogue he might be, but at least he was being an open one. He did indeed lay his cards on the table—and a very grubby pack they were: though, as Mr. Billing himself pointed out with a wry laugh, all cards get soiled when you play with 'em!

Yes, indeed, Mr. Billing and the two men in brown had once been concerned with each other . . .

"Did they *'ave* to kill the old man?" muttered Smith, dismally. "Were it necessary?"

The attorney shrugged his shoulders.

"Ask Mister Green, my friend."

Smith shivered, and once more his blood was uncannily chilled.

"W-was he the *other* one? The one I heard? The one with the limp?"

"More than a limp, Smith. A wooden leg. Very soft-spoken man. Very devilish. I don't think I'd like to meet with Mister Green on a dark night!"

The attorney paused—and looked uneasily about him, as if he expected soft-spoken Mr. Green to limp out of a shadow and knife him where he sat.

"Right, my lad! I'll lay my cards on the table—" (Here, Smith wondered, bemusedly, whether this was the same pack or a second one.)

"That document's worth money. A vast deal of money. Enough for you and me and the chimney sweep down the road! Hm! I mean our friend, Mister Green. For I tell you, young man, I see no way of keeping him out of it. None! He's got the pair of us, Smith! We're the little running rats, and he's the gobbling devil! If only, Smith—ah! if only—"

"If only what, Mister Billing?"

"You and me . . . just you and me . . . Where did you leave the document?"

"In—" began Smith, then something distracted him: the fettered old man. Was he having a fit? He was banging his chained wrists down on the floor.

"Where, Smith? Where?"

But Smith had suddenly thought more deeply.

"Lorst me memory, Mister Billing."

"What d'you mean?"

"Strain of waiting to be nubbed, Mister Billing. Can't remember a thing. Leastways, not while I'm 'ere."

"Don't you trust me, friend?"

Smith stared into the attorney's reproachful face and slowly shook his head.

"No, Mister Billing. I've had enough of trust to last me the rest of me life."

A dreadful bitterness had come back into Smith's small pointed face, making it seem as old as the hills. Mr. Billing's smooth cheeks seemed to pale somewhat. He murmured something about Smith "sleeping on it," and that he'd see him tomorrow. Then he stood up and began to move away, trying to hold Smith's eyes in his own unchanging ones till the shuffling ragbag of Newgate inhabitants got between him and his prey.

For long minutes Smith stared after him, not moving till he was taken up with the sounds of a commotion that seemed to be flowing, like seedy blood, through the prison's veins. A rumor. Dick Mulrone had been pardoned! But even before that rumor had gone its rounds, its contradiction was already at its heels. No pardon. Poor Dick Mulrone's prospects were like a wave in the sea—forever followed by its trough. Twelve more days remained to him: and Mr. Jones, being Welsh and tuneful and fanciful, had already begun his Tyburn Carol:

> On the first day of counting
> My true love sent to me
> A felon in an elm tree.

"That's my boy!" wheezed the old man, recovered from his fit. "Like a blooming nightingale!"

NOT LONG BEFORE, there'd been set up on Newgate's roof a great windmill with vanes a full twenty feet across. Its purpose was to purify the air. As it turned it drew up (by natural suction and skilful design), through tubes and tunnels joining into a middle shaft, much of the foul and pestilential vapors of the Jail . . . which, some said, hovered thereafter like a green patch on the sky.

In the setting up of this engine, certain old ventilators had been cleaned out, and into one of them a drunken workman had dropped his wig. Drunkenly, he'd ordered his apprentice to go down and fetch it. Which, after much jeering and persuasion, the boy had done. The dreadful stench nearly killed him, and he fell into what was feared to be the jail fever. He was taken to St. Thomas's Hospital where he remained in a delirium till he died, swearing that he'd seen in the ventilator a bald man with spectacles and a cruel smile whom he straightway recognized as the Devil, a-catching the souls of prisoners as the windmill sucked them up.

After this, the Devil was seen pretty often in Newgate, his pockets stuffed with contracts for debtors' souls. Felons, it seemed, he didn't bother with overmuch, as it was supposed they'd disposed of their souls to him long before and so had nothing else to mortgage; but among the debtors, they say, he did a roaring trade. Men like Mr. Palmer were ever on the look out for him—and often might be seen driving desperate bargains with bald men with spectacles. Women and children he was also interested in—particularly children.

In his first nights in Newgate Smith dreamed many times of the Devil, and what terms he might get for his soul. He had long conversations with him, in which the Devil offered him escape, vengeance on the Mansfields, and enough of money for himself, Mr. Billing, *and* the chimney sweep down the road. And all for a little future frying—

"I like you, Smith," the Devil murmured. "We're both men of the world and I'm partial to you. Particularly fried."

Which prospect didn't seem as horrible as it might have, for nights in Stone Hall were that dismal and cold that the thought of any fire—even Hell's—was agreeable. Also, these nights were unnaturally long and hard to sleep in. There were continual mutterings and mumblings and sudden cryings out. There was the clinking of leg irons which sounded—when it was regular—like an endless chain

being winched into some deep pit. While from far off—
from that part of the Jail that was called "The Castle,"
where wealthy felons and prisoners of state paid high
money for their lodging—came the faint sounds of singing
and good cheer as Dick Mulrone was swigged and swilled
on his way to his end.

> On the fourth day of counting
> My true love sent to me
> Four sextons digging,
> Three parsons praying,
> Two horses drawing,
> And a felon in an elm tree.

On which, Smith's ancient fireplace companion would
moan and wheeze and finally wake up with a "That's my
boy!" and jingle into a sitting position from which he'd
watch Smith with deceiving bright eyes.

"Looking for the Newgate star?" he'd begin: for Smith
usually lay with his eyes wide open and fixed on the
ragged black hole above.

Then the old man would mumble and mutter about
Smith's visitors and what they'd had to say. He missed
nothing, and it seemed, at times, as if picking up scraps of
other folks' business was the only thing that kept him
alive.

Of all Smith's visitors, he was most inquisitive about
Mr. Billing, whom he regarded as a "real caution of a
gent" and "one to be handled with the tongs."

Mr. Billing had come to see Smith every day, sometimes
only for minutes, but at other times for an hour or more.
Once, he met Miss Bridget and Miss Fanny and exchanged the briefest of courtesies with them; then left
almost directly, saying he'd be out of place in family dis-

cussions. Miss Fanny was much impressed by him, and even Miss Bridget had to admit he was "quite gentlemanly to the look." All of which gave Smith a certain gloomy pride—though he never admitted to more than "legal business" between himself and the visiting attorney and so left his sisters most respectfully puzzled. But no matter whether Mr. Billing stayed long or short, he contrived to strengthen his acquaintance with Smith by unexpected touches of humor and warmth.

He scarce ever referred to the document again, but seemed to regard the matter as being settled between them. Once or twice he spoke of Mr. Green, but it was only to say that thank God! that evil man had not shown himself. Also, he begged Smith to be on his guard against such a visitor, though he doubted if Mr. Green would dare to show his face in Newgate . . . He hinted also of "a departure from this place to pastures new" . . . which was being thought of, never fear! Was the other matter, likewise in hand? To which Smith had nodded very gloomily indeed.

This sadness of his had been carefully observed by the ancient eavesdropper who taxed Smith with it that night.

"You ain't got it, have you!" he said triumphantly.

"Got what?"

"What he wants. So you'll have to stay!"

He looked pleased as punch at the thought of Smith being his companion forever.

"You mind yer own business!" muttered Smith, savagely, and glared the old man's beam off his face.

"Ain't got none to mind," said the old man, forlornly, and Smith relented somewhat and explained dismally:

"If I stays, they'll nub me!"

But the old man seemed not to've heard him for he

stared vacantly into the air for several minutes: then slowly closed up his eyes and went to sleep still sitting, and leaving Smith to worry himself into a state of sick desperation.

His trial was already fixed. January twenty-third was the day: the very day they were nubbing Dick Mulrone. "Swing out the old, swing in the new" so to speak . . .

Smith came to thinking his fate and Mr. Mulrone's were somehow linked, and if the highwayman perished he'd not be long after. Eight more days had Dick Mulrone. How many had Smith?

The document! The cursed document! Furiously, he shut his eyes and tried to picture it, hoping his new skill in reading would reveal—from his mind's eye—what Mr. Billing wanted to know. But alas! he could make no more of it now then when he'd looked at it in his darkest ignorance. His mind's eye showed him nothing but a spidery jumble. For, not having understood what he'd seen, he'd not known what to remember . . . and not all the fierce screwings up of his face (to the old man's consternation and grief) brought it one whit the clearer or nearer.

Now he wondered if Miss Mansfield had come upon the document yet—and if it had meant anything to her. He sweated with terror at the thought of her giving it to the attorney for nothing! Then a queer thought struck him. If the old gentleman had been on his way to the attorney's anyway, why had he been waylaid? Why hadn't the attorney waited for the document to be laid in his lap? Or would it have been laid in Mr. Lennard's lap—and would that have been fatal to his design? Or, still more likely, was there a darker mystery yet concerning the connection with the limping Mr. Green?

"Oh Gawd!" whispered Smith, staring up into the

blackness of the chimney as if for an answer. "Why did the old gent 'ave to stuff his pockets with sich deadly papers? What right 'ad 'e to go stumping through the streets, heavy with the Devil's literature for to tempt the likes of me with?"

He shook his head, and groaned and groaned at the misery of his lot—and wondered if he'd be hanged without ever discovering what he was being hanged for.

Smith's hopes were low. Only one had held out any promise, and even that one had so far failed him. Till the Sunday. And then at last, she came. Meg, the scullery maid from Vine Street.

She'd kept her word even through a heavy fall of snow that had begun during the night and was not yet done with. Her shawl and bonnet were grandly dappled with flakes and her nose had been whipped by the wind to a strawberry . . . but she'd brought Smith some veal pie, sausage, and white bread. Also two shirts he'd left behind.

"You pore thing," she said, giving him the bundle. "Oh you pore thing!" She gazed at him sadly. "You've grown smaller and wizened. You needs feeding up, and—not meaning to be personal, dear—you needs another good wash!"

Smith shuddered at the memory, and began to unwrap his bundle while Meg looked about her at the skinny, blotched, and sadly cunning faces that haunted the Stone Hall.

"Cleverness?" she sniffed. "Look where it gets you! I'll wager there's enough cleverness here to sink London Bridge! Brains? Give you a farthing for 'em!"

Then she settled down with a great commotion of her bonnet and shawl and began to talk of the changes for the worse in Vine Street since Smith had gone. Mr. Mansfield, it seemed, hardly had a civil word for anybody, and the mistress was a regular demon, finding fault where there was none . . . which Meg considered was a demon's chief office. Even handsome Mr. Billing wasn't particularly welcome for, try as he might to be cheerful of an evening, the talk always came back to Smith: and there was an end of all cheerfulness. Meg said this with some satisfaction, as if it ought to've been a real comfort to Smith to learn he was the cause of misery. But Smith nodded and smiled, and smiled and nodded—and bided his time. Till at last, through all the byways of her conversation, Meg came back to "You pore thing!" with the sigh of someone who's been the long way round.

Smith said: "They're a-going to 'ang me, Meg."

"Oh, you pore thing!"

"There's but one soul who can save me, Meg."

"Ah! the master!"

"No, Meg, *you*!"

Meg looked astonished: fidgeted with the fringe of her shawl, then slowly shook her head with an air of great sadness.

"If heart can save you, child, then it's done. But this is a wicked world of cleverness . . ."

"It's heart I need, Meg—for it's cleverness what put me 'ere!"

Meg nodded deeply. That was no less than the truth.

"Say on, little one."

So Smith bent close and began to mutter urgently and pleadingly in Meg's large, gentle ear. Did she recall the paper she'd found when he'd been washed? She nodded.

Was it still where she'd put it? Most likely . . . most likely: it had been deep in a drawer.

Could she get at it? Most likely—

Would she get at it—for Smith?

She opened her eyes in alarm. "Why, child! It's the master's!"

"No! It was mine! And it's the only thing that'll save me!"

"I—I couldn't steal from the master!"

"But it was mine—"

"—It's all a nasty piece of cleverness, child! You'd be best off without it! Believe Meg!"

"Meg-Meg! You're a-hanging me! True as we're 'ere! If I don't get it, I'll be buried afore the Spring! Meg—"

"Oh little one . . . oh . . ."

The frightened Meg had begun to cry with the sudden misery of her dilemma. Her heart and conscience were much at odds. More than ever, she hated cleverness and all it brought in its sly train.

"I—I don't know what to do! Oh Lord! what would me mother have said?"

As she rocked herself to and fro (and was mistook by several sneering debtors for Smith's own mother, weeping over her felonious brat), the old man began to rock himself likewise—and then croaked, amazingly like the parrot he so closely resembled: "Meg! Meg! Follow your heart! Meg!"

She looked startled—then stared with wet eyes at the disreputable old man. She nodded.

"That's her voice, child: and them's her words. For she often talks to me now she's dead and gone. Sometimes out of old men, sometimes out of mischievous urchins—and sometimes out of heaps of potato peelings! And it's always, 'Follow your heart, Meg!' So I'll fetch you the paper, little Smith—and may it save yore poor neck from the shameful noose!"

Smith considered himself as good as out of the Jail: and the change in him was as astonishing as it was abrupt. His spirits rose and he put on a confident, almost patronizing air. He strutted importantly about the dismal Stone Hall, even finding opportunities to practice his reading upon the scratched messages, prayers, and rages that scarred the damp walls. "God have mercy on me," he read out: and shrugged his shoulders. Next, he read: "Jo loves Bess." He scratched his head and wondered why anybody should want to write such a thing on a prison wall. Then, "God rot all lawyers." Hm! That was more like it!

His high spirits were bewildering to his sisters who'd last seen him in the depths of gloom.

"Oh Smut!" said Miss Fanny. "To see you in such spirits is better than a pint of gin, dear! Now, no matter what befalls, we'll know you went happy!"

"Oh, I'll be 'appy going!" said Smith, enigmatically; and Miss Bridget stared at him sadly, as if he was a lost soul.

But Mr. Billing understood. Maybe at first he wondered if Smith had the document already . . . for he'd arrived shortly after Meg had left. Not that it was really likely he'd seen her—there being such a stew in Newgate at that time, what with Mulrone's visitors and the bad weather . . . But he saw the bundle and smiled knowingly. Smith, seeing this look, divined its meaning. He shook his head and grinned.

"Not yet, Mister Billing! But it won't be long before the chimney sweep down the road'll be situated to buy himself new brooms and a whole new chimney for his very own! If you take my meaning, Mister Billing!"

Mr. Billing took his meaning.

"And it won't be long before a certain little bird flies out of its stone cage, eh, lad?" He beamed and laid his hand on Smith's thin shoulder.

"How much better it is to put our cards on the table—play fair . . . and be friends! Oh the world's not such a bad place after all—for the likes of you and me!"

This was on Sunday, January fourteen: a day remembered, if for no other reason than for the extraordinary violence and passion of its snowstorm. It was as if the Devil's cat had got among the angels and was scattering their feathers everywhere. There seemed no end to the snow . . .

chapter TWELVE

THE SNOW CONTINUED to fall . . . sometimes in great
whirling quantities, and sometimes—for half a day at
a stretch—in idle, drifting flakes that wafted wearily down
as if the air was filled with invisible obstructions, then
added themselves imperceptibly to the general whiteness
below.

The worn old streets were gone: the blackened roof
tiles were gone: the mournful chimneys and the dirty posts
wore high white hats—and the houses themselves seemed
to float, muffled, in a sea of white. Never, in all its life, had
the Town looked so clean: it shamed the very sky, which
was of a dirty, yellowish gray.

The business of the Town was slow and tedious: car-

riages and chairs crawled along where they supposed were
the streets, like huge, tottery snails, bearing snow houses
on their backs and leaving wet black trails to mark their
passing. Even the nimble piemen capered silently, sometimes slipped and lost their smoking trays so that half a
hundred hot pies burned into the snow and pitted it like a
black pox . . .

Visitors to Newgate Jail were few and far between.
Only the loving and hardy called. Dick Mulrone's friends
were much diminished, and it was said he grew scornful
and sour and melancholy. And Smith, waiting for Meg,
grew uneasy: there was no snow inside of Newgate, so the
traveling troubles of the world seemed as remote as the
stars. Only his sisters and the ever faithful Mr. Billing
came to see him, and, once in a while, Lord Tom. For, in
these days, Lord Tom spent a deal of time with his
doomed colleague whose room, being less crowded,
offered more space for Lord Tom to be noticed and welcomed. After which, smelling strongly of wine, and with a
kind of swaggering stagger, the green-cloaked high toby
would look in briefly on Smith and give him the news of
"glorious Dick."

"He's hopes," said Lord Tom, with a mournful grin, "of
the snow piling so high under the Tree that, when the cart
drives off, he'll be left standing instead of the horrible
swing!"

Smith nodded: and was not above being grateful for his
friend's efforts to be companionable. Then his abstracted
air returned as he tried hard to imagine what was preventing Meg. There was now little time left—for Thursday
came and went without a sniff of her. Smith fancied Mr.
Billing was growing suspicious and impatient, and it
seemed plain he'd do nothing about the escape till he was

sure he'd benefit. He said nothing of any plan, even though he was always true enough to his own queer nature and remained amiable. Nonetheless, he spoke no more of "laying cards on the table," but somehow contrived to make it plain that it was now his young friend's place to do that very thing. Which Smith was in no position to oblige. Whether or not the attorney conceived this uneasy silence to be a duel of nerves and wits was hard to say: but it was possible he did and overestimated the boy, else something happened which made him change his mind.

On the Friday he met Smith with a rueful and disarming smile, which Smith returned with a look of such deep and earnest hope that stonier hearts than Mr. Billing's (if any there were) would have been melted by it. He shook his head and laughed and murmured something about "Smith's winning," and "friendship coming before all." Then he sat down, and to Smith's amazement, relief, and delight, confided the plan for the escape!

How was it to be done? The ventilators. The grated apertures in the walls. The narrow tunnels that led, through dark and angled ways, to the great shaft that rose up to the windmill on the roof. From which grimy eminence it was but a hop, a jump, and a scramble to the nestage of adjoining roofs.

With beating heart and glittering eyes Smith listened as the attorney muttered rapidly on. Dipping his finger fastidiously in Smith's ale, he drew on the table-top a plan of the wards and halls of the Jail alongside of which the ventages ran. Very narrow were the lower tunnels—only wide enough to admit a thin child. But on the next floor they were somewhat more spacious and roughly bricked so's to afford finger and toe holds for "little birds to reach the sky."

Wider and wider were these tunnels constructed, till at last they came into the main shaft that rose, like a soul in Grace, to the windmill and the heavens. Upward, always upward must the little bird go—else, ha-ha, he'd find himself in another cage!

Carefully, he wiped his finger on his handkerchief and Smith stared at the shining lines and squares that were beginning now to pool and dry and lose their powerful meaning. But they were already well fixed in his mind. He nodded, and looked up for the last question. When was he to go? Not yet. Why? The grating was not yet unlocked. The good offices of a certain gentleman (here, Mr. Billing looked about him quickly) were not yet bespoke. But never fear, they would be. When? On the Tuesday. Why so long? Not so long: only four more days. But why not Monday? Ah! Tuesday would be a day of great commotion. Dick Mulrone would be setting forth. Jailers and turnkeys would be busied in keeping order—and too busy to notice a little bird fly out of its cage! Tuesday, at six o'clock—before Smith would have been moved to the sessions' house for his trial. Tuesday. Freedom day! Mr. Billing grinned . . . document day!

Smith's wavering spirits lifted and he stared long and hard at the ventilator grating that was let into the wall beside the fireplace. But even now, it was impossible to rid himself of all of a thousand uncanny fears of disasters pouncing before the Tuesday. Yet—Mr. Billing had been confident . . . and Mr. Billing was nobody's fool. All that remained, then, was the visit from Meg with the document. Surely, she'd not fail him! Not Meg with her monstrous great heart!

She didn't fail him. Or, at least, not entirely. She came

on the following day. Her shawl, bonnet, skirts, and shoes were loaded with snow; she'd walked the whole way and the effort had made her steam, so that there was a general meltingness about her. Her hair, eyebrows, nose, and chin all seemed to be discharging water, which gave her red face a curiously dismayed air.

"A glass of gin, Meg?" said Smith, anxiously, as she dripped into the tap room.

She shivered and shook her head . . . and seemed unwilling to sit down. Suddenly, Smith—with a dreadful fear —saw that her dismay was more than snow deep. Her customarily round face was oval—and her eyes were unnaturally red.

"'ave you—'ave you got it, Meg?"

She stared at him in terrified sorrow, as if imploring him to hold his peace.

"Meg! Where is it?"

"Oh child! Oh little one! They'll hang you now for sure! And bury you afore the Spring! Oh, you pore thing!"

"Meg! Where is it?"

"Heart weren't enough, little one! Horrible cleverness is all! Brains? Lord! I wish I had 'em!"

"Where is it?"

She dabbed at her nose with her sleeve and her whole face grew veiled with fearful memories.

"On Thursday . . . yes, the Thursday, the master and mistress went out together: so I took me chance, little one, and crept like a mouse to the study—"

Smith, the first shock of dread spent, listened in a sick dismay. What had gone so grievously awry?

"I was in the very room, child—the very room—"

She repeated herself, as if to prove her heart had ever been twice as strong as any circumstance.

"—when I heard a noise, child, from upstairs. From upstairs where you used to sleep! Oh Lord, dear! I thought —I feared you'd lost patience and gone from the Jail and come back on your own desperate account! I was worried half out of me mind! I thought of calling out to you . . . then I thought it'd frighten you off. So, quiet as a mouse— as a mouse, I crept out and went up them dreadful stairs. Sure enough, there was noise coming from your own dear room. But queer noise. Scraping—dragging—pulling— panting . . . like it was being torn apart by dumb beasts! Lord! Lord! I was that frightened! I thought maybe a bear had got in!"

"What was it, Meg?" whispered Smith—though maybe he'd guessed . . .

"I screamed, child! That I did! Screamed and shrieked till Vine Street echoed! I got a good pair of lungs, child— a good pair of lungs!"

"And—then?"

"It must have scared 'em!"

"Who?"

"Two horrible men in brown! They burst out of the room in a terrible rage! I thought they'd kill me—but they rushed past me and down the stairs then out through the front door like the wind o' Hell!"

"The Thursday? This was on—on the Thursday, Meg?"

Meg stared at him vaguely, as if wondering why the day should have mattered so much. For among all the wild and panic-stricken thoughts that had whirled through Smith's head, one had stuck fast. On the day following that Thursday, the attorney had come to him with a rueful smile—a smile that Smith suddenly knew was of disappointment! And he'd said Smith had won. Indeed, he'd won! The men in brown had failed!

(Meg's voice bobbed on, dwelling on all the consequences of the breaking-in, for it filled her poor head to distraction.)

And because they'd failed, the attorney had come to see him, cap in hand, with the plan for the escape! "You've won, Smith!" had meant exactly that! And now . . .

"So there's no more hope, little one!" said Meg, with the grandmother of all sighs.

"No more 'ope?"

Smith looked at her, bewildered—having missed what she'd thought was the chief part of her bad news. Which, with a groan, she repeated. The burglary had so alarmed Mr. Mansfield that he'd locked all his papers securely away. There was now no hope in the world of getting at them . . .

"Oh child! They'll hang you now—and Meg, heart and all, won't be able to stop 'em! Why, child—you're a-smiling! Why, little one—you're a-grinning! Why, Smith, dear—you ain't downhearted! Oh God bless you, dear, for not breaking Meg's heart with your despairing! You'll go straight to Heaven, Smith—no matter *what* you done!"

For Smith, in spite of the evil news, was smiling in the most strangely excited way: and when at last she went, promising that she'd try to do something, no matter what, to save him, he called loudly after her:

"Thank you, Meg! Truly, thank you! You've saved me life!" Which was like Sunday bells in her ears!

Even the old man had been surprised, and he'd thought himself long past such sensations. But Smith, saying nothing, grinned most knowingly. Aggravated, the old man shuffled close beside him.

"You've not got it yet, have you?"

"No. I ain't. But nor 'as 'e!"

"So what are you grinning for? And why did you thank that sloppy baggage?"

"Because that lawyer's got ears as long as Watling Street—and I'd like 'im to think I'm pleased!"

The old man chuckled. No matter what the cause, he enjoyed folk being misled.

" 'e thought 'e'd have me for 'is dinner," went on Smith, his face darkening with knowledgable contempt. " 'e thought I was that easy! Oh! the crafty lawyer, 'im!"

The old man grinned. He liked to hear of scoundrelly behaviors. Very satisfying, he found it.

"And 'is friends in brown! Wish I'd seen their faces! Wish I'd seen 'is face when they told 'im what luck they'd 'ad!"

The old man agreed. *He'd* liked to've seen such a multiplication of dismay. He enjoyed dismay.

"And picture 'is oily face now—when 'e hears simple little Smith has just thanked Meg 'eartily! 'Tom Billing,' 'e'll say, 'you got to help that lad, for it stands to reason 'e's got the document already. Else why did 'e thank that sloppy baggage?' Oh yes! Picture 'is face!"

The old man pictured it—and seemed to enjoy that most of all. The two of them—the old man not much bigger than Smith—sat grinning at each other across the mournful fireplace like a pair of goblin firedogs . . .

"Won't be long now," said the old man, jerking his head toward the ventilator: and Smith felt an odd pang of regret—even shame—that he'd be escaping and the old man would not. But the old man didn't seem to mind. Indeed, he seemed quite gay at the thought for, though there were many things he liked much better, he was quite partial to the idea of the occasional little bird flying off.

Not that there was any remarkable sympathy, or any mysterious bond of friendship, between these two strongly differing prisoners. There was nothing in common between them save the fireplace: and even there, each maintained his own side and scowled pretty formidably if there was any encroachment by the other.

"What d'you want? A whole bleeding *park*?" the offended one would mutter: and the trespasser would sniff and move back again. Then there'd be silence between them for several minutes while they watched the fierce and dingy residents of Stone Hall going about their endless, purposeless business . . . like dirty water round a choked drain . . .

God knows what the old man thought as he gazed at his eternal neighbors to whom each day was as a year (with but a single season), and yesterday was as a thousand years gone and of no more account. He must have had some thoughts—for every man has thoughts, be they ever so dark—but maybe they were too awkward for words, like the prints left by a bird in the sky . . .

Even Smith's thoughts were vague and shiftable. The confidence of his escaping gave him both a superior feeling toward those who could not—and a queer affection. His time among them (he was firmly convinced) could now be counted in hours. Till something happened on the Monday evening that frightened the wits out of him and filled those last hours with commotion and dread!

"Visitor!" croaked the old man, sharpishly. "Look lively! Visitor!"

Smith looked up—and was at once struck with astonishment and apprehension! The visitor was Miss Mansfield!

What had brought her—at this late stage and through

snow and searing weather—to come and stare down, angrily and passionately, at the "little murderer?"

A terrible feeling that Mr. Billing had confided the plan to Miss Mansfield and she, in a righteous rage, had come to wreck it, chilled his heart. He could conceive of no other reason. His eyes glittered desperately.

"Smith!" cried Miss Mansfield, throwing back her hood and staring about her with lively horror and shame. "You've grown vastly dirty again!"

"Mister Jones won't mind—"

"—who's he?"

"The 'angman!"

Impulsively, Miss Mansfield knelt down, stretched out her arms (careless of her cloak, whose yellow lining flashed out, abrupt as a flower), and took Smith's shoulders.

"Keep off! Keep off!" he cried fearfully—black memories of his last day on Vine Street clutching at his heart . . . and the eerie feeling that Miss Mansfield was come on a worse errand than to tell him he was dirty. This feeling was exceedingly strong, and set up a shivering through all of his thin body.

Miss Mansfield—as ever mistress of all but her own face—scowled ferociously and tried to blink away some tears. She turned to the old man who was watching with abiding interest.

"I-I would help him—"

" 'e don't need your 'elp, ma'am."

Smith, by now, was almost up the chimney in his fright.

"What d'you want with me? Keep off! Leave me alone! I 'ate you . . ."

The pain that Smith was inflicting was out of all proportion to his small size. His revenge on the Saint of Vine

Street—did he but know it—was complete indeed. The lady's face had so distraught and tormented an aspect that even the sneering watchers were struck by it. Her heart was in a very pitiful state, being pierced by the sharpest of arrows: self-blame. She did indeed blame herself—for indulging her blind father's mania for justice at the expense of the shivering, terrified child who now shrank away from her. She was not—nor ever had been—lacking in compassion, but she'd dispensed it unequally—and now suffered accordingly. Though she'd come to the Jail to tell Smith something, she could not overcome her own distress sufficiently to say more than:

"Smith . . . child . . . I-I would help . . . Don't hate us, I beg of you! Smith—Smith—"

But Smith glared and glared, morbidly convinced that the mad daughter of the mad father was come as a harbinger of doom.

Which, in a way, she was. There was a disturbance at the other end of the Hall. Turnkeys were shouting: the seething, irritable crowd was being pushed and chevvied. It moved this way and that like a Red Sea that would not part. Till at last it did part, falling away somewhat savagely from a tremendous figure who'd been caught in its midst, despite the turnkeys who'd been beating at the felons and debtors and shouting:

"Blind man! Blind man! Make way—"

It was Mr. Mansfield! Blind as night . . . helplessly upright . . . his black spectacles in the great gloom looking more than ever like deep holes in his head. The turnkeys pushed obstructions from his path and led him, with many an important scowl at the resentful crowd, toward the fireplace.

Miss Mansfield looked alarmed and angry. She'd left

her father in the carriage. Bade him not come in. Said she'd accomplish all without interference or help . . . So why *had* he come, with that strange, desperate look about his mouth that disturbed her violently?

"Here you are, your honor!" said one of the guiding turnkeys—and grinned awkwardly while waiting for the blind man to fish in his pocket for a coin. Maybe he hoped for a guinea in mistake for a shilling? But the coin proved to be a halfpenny and the turnkey—under Miss Mansfield's strong frown—retreated with a contemptuous, "No fee, your honor. Not from a blind man!"

"Daughter—"

"Yes, sir—"

The blind man nodded and seemed to stare at the wall . . . as if, even to his useless eyes, the horror, darkness, degradation, and shame of the Stone Hall was a sight not to be endured.

"Is—he—here?"

"Yes, sir."

"Smith," said Mr. Mansfield, quietly. "Do you know what this is?"

He thrust his hand into his coat and drew out—THE DOCUMENT!

A sound between a scream and a groan told Mr. Mansfield that Smith knew.

"Meg told us," murmured Miss Mansfield, painfully. "In tears, she came, poor soul! At her wits' end. Said it was the only thing that would save you . . ."

"Do you know what it is, Smith?"

"No! No! Never seen it before!"

"Look again. Look closely. Look hard."

Helplessly, Smith looked. Yellower and more stained than he remembered . . . smaller, even . . . but it was the document. Now he could read on the outside: "To Mister Lennard. Billing and Lennard of Curtis Court, Godliman Street."

Frantically, he eyes strove to pierce the fold in the paper and read what was within. But in vain. He had a mad idea of snatching it! But where could he fly? Up the chimney?

"Never-seen-it-before!" he repeated: but his voice was harsh and unequal.

Mr. Mansfield put the paper away—and Smith's eyes crawled after it, into the vital pocket where all was black as night.

"Mister Lennard is at Prickler's Hill. I'm taking this document to him, Smith."

"W-what's in it, then?"

"I—I do not know. It is for Mister Lennard. A dead man's wish, Smith. Binding. No arguing with it. It shall be delivered. Tomorrow."

"And let's hope and pray, Smith," said Miss Mansfield, still kneeling, "that it will indeed save you."

"Tomorrow," went on Mr. Mansfield, "Mister Billing will apply for an adjournment of your trial. I have asked him . . ."

"Then 'e knows?" This was meant for a whisper, but it came out very near a scream.

"He knows no more than I've told him. Why should he? This is Mister Lennard's affair."

" 'e knows—'e knows!" moaned Smith, now in his blackest extremity, for it seemed to him that the evil document was coming full circle! He knew for certain that blind Mr. Mansfield was as marked and doomed a soul as had been Mr. Field!

All Smith's hatred and feelings for revenge sank abruptly in a sea of pity. The two men in brown would waylay the magistrate and murder him! And so at last they'd have what they'd been paid to get: and maybe Mr. Green would thank them in his soft voice . . . In his mind's eye, Smith could already see the look on Mr. Mansfield's face as his soul left his body: and it was the selfsame look he'd seen in Curtis Court . . .

"You blind old fool!" he wept furiously. "They'll kill you! You old madman! Blind, blind, blind right through you are!"

But Mr. Mansfield and his daughter were already moving, and the turnkeys were clearing their path. Men stared at the blind Justice hostilely . . . shook their fists at him, made threatening faces—and sometimes jeered. Someone —for the turnkeys were not overcareful, now—managed to push his foot out so's the blind man staggered and nearly fell: but his daughter gripped hold on his arm and steadied him—in body, if not in spirit . . .

When they were gone Smith looked dismally about for a certain fish-eyed jailer whom, he had reason to believe, was the one who retailed everything to Mr. Billing and had most likely been paid to unlock the grating. His heart quickened. The man was nowhere to be seen. He had not been present. Was it still possible, then, that the escape would go forward? That the jailer would do what he'd been paid for without further reference to his employer? Or had Mr. Billing already summoned him and grimly shook his head? Scarce eighteen hours remained . . .

A STRANGE NIGHT, much given over to restlessness and rumors about Dick Mulrone. Rumors that he'd nubbed himself to cheat Mr. Jones: rumors that he'd been reprieved and was dead drunk on that score: rumors that he'd changed clothes with a visitor and gone out as the Duchess of Newcastle: rumors that twenty of his roistering friends were broke in, armed with pistols, muskets, and poniards, for to whisk him back to the freedom of Hounslow Heath where coaches lumbered in their dozens, overripe for the plucking . . .

Then, between midnight and dawn, the easy voice of Mr. Jones, the hangman, put a stop to it all:

On the last day of counting
My true love sent to me:
Twelve jurors juggling,
Eleven clerks a-counting,
Ten friends a-failing,
Nine dead men . . .
Eight widows weeping,
Seven judges judging,
Six drummers drumming,
Five yards of rope . . .
Four sextons digging,
Three parsons praying,
Two horses drawing—
And a felon in an elm tree.

"That's my boy!" mumbled the old man—and leaned over to dig his companion in the ribs. But Smith had at last gone to sleep, so the old man desisted and rocked himself to and fro, humming the tune of the Tyburn Carol as softly as a lullaby, and gently clinking his fetters in time, so that the tune and the jingling might have sounded like Christmas harness in a dreaming ear . . .

But at a quarter of six—or thereabouts—the old man shook Smith and bade him be gone.

The Stone Hall was dark and quiet still—as a consequence of the disturbed night. Probably, no one was awake save the old man and the furtive boy.

"Up on me back!" breathed the old man—and knelt so's Smith might mount on that bony eminence to reach the grating.

"What if it ain't unlocked?" whispered Smith, full of last minute dreads and alarms.

"It's been done."

"When?"

"While you slept. I heard. I saw. Come now—up! Up! Up!"

Smith paused. "D'you think you could come too?"

"Don't want to. This is me home. Got company."

Smith nodded. He shook the old man's hand.

"I'll not be seeing you more—"

"—I hopes not! Up you go!"

Smith hoisted himself onto the old man's back which was as hard and steady as a rock.

" 'ope you gets a gentleman for the fireplace what suits—"

"—that's my affair!"

"No offense—"

"—none took. In you go, you scabby little sparrow!"

Smith had opened the grating. The air within was thick and damp and laden with evil smells. For a moment he thought the vent was too narrow even for him. Then he pushed with his feet against the old man's back and felt, first his shoulders, then his arms, elbows, and hips scrape the rough stone walls . . .

"You're in!" he heard the old man whisper. "Best of luck—and watch out for . . ."

Smith never heard what he was to watch out for as all sound behind him was lost in the eerie sighing of the prison's secret lungs. This sighing was as regular as breathing itself—and a thousand times more foul . . . for high up on the roof, the windmill was motionless under a muffling blockage of snow . . .

A hundred and fifty feet of rough, uncanny darkness, divided into three steep channels, lay between Smith and the last great shaft. At the juncture of each of these channels, once jagged but now smooth and somewhat slippery apertures were let in: these led to other parts of the Jail and furnished Smith with foot-and-fingerholds to heave himself round each sharp bend and continue his upward burrowing. That he *was* moving upward he knew chiefly by the direction of his own sweat which ran continually into his eyes . . . not that those organs were of much use, for the darkness was formidable and absolute.

"So what was I to watch out for?" he muttered, ironically. "Black rats? Black cats?"

The sound of his own voice cheered him and henceforward he mocked his own trembling spirits aloud. With a curious effect of which he had no knowledge: his mumbling, muttering tones traveled weirdly through devious passages and stony veins till they were wafted into the deepest and most dreadful parts of the Jail.

A man in the Pressroom—on whom were weights past bearing—heard faintly:

"Come on, now, me boy! Give in? Not you, me sweeting! What's a bruised belly between friends? On with you! Up with you—to the waiting 'eavens!"

But other jailbirds, in their remote cages, heard, maybe, nothing so apt and heartening. Curses and abuse of the prison's scope and architecture came out of the various gratings—as if Newgate was alive to its own wretchedness and was at last complaining aloud. Then (in the King's Bench Ward):

"Be off with you, you fat, wicked 'orror! What are you waiting for? Dinner? Be off or I'll bite your 'orrible 'ead off!"

Smith and a rat. He'd met it by a nest of vents, its eyes gleaming in some vague, wandering light. It had come from a deeper channel and now stopped, amazed, to watch what it took to be a grand relation, passing bulkily by . . .

"Upways, downways, in me lady's chamber! Which way now? Lost! 'Up,' he said. But which way's up? Where's the sky? Which of these dismal ways is the one to 'eaven? Come, me old friend! Try this fair stinker! Feet first—as they says in the trade!"

This, heard in My Lady's Hold, caused much terror and consternation: but further on, the wandering voice (believed by some to be that of a walled-in ghost) was not so gay. It complained horribly of bruises and swellings got from scrapes and pressures against the ragged, bulging walls. It complained of having taken a wrong turn and finding itself, baffled and helpless, staring through bars into a cage more desolate than the one that had been left. It seemed to be losing heart under the strain of an intolerable journey. So miserable did the voice become at this point, that those who heard it were moved almost to tears by a plight they had no notion of, and whispered:

"Whatever you are—wherever you are—for God's sake cheer up—and the best of luck!"

Maybe this had reached its mark? At all events nothing more was heard of the traveling voice, and the iron-barred vents were as silent as the grave.

What had happened? Smith had come into the last great shaft: the broad-ribbed, secret gullet that led (like a soul in Grace) to the windmill and the sky!

Bruised and much fouled from his journeying, he crouched in the last bend and stared triumphantly up. Fifteen feet above him hung the motionless vanes of the windmill, folded in snow. And then the sky: gray and

weighty and still dispensing its flakes which flickered down and down and down—even kissing Smith's upturned face.

A tremendous moment. Not the Dean of St. Paul's had a finer view to Heaven, nor a more heartfelt gaze at the sky. Smith began to climb . . .

He stopped. There was an oddness, a queerness about the lip of the shaft. A ragged irregularity. Which seemed to be growing subtly. Like a pair of plague swellings . . .

A sudden gust of wind whipped a veil of snow across his vision: then it was gone and the two swellings were most marked. What were they? Heads. Two men. A pair of hands reached down. Fingers twitched and beckoned . . .

In the sudden and terrible agony of his betrayal, Smith screamed aloud! Looking down upon him, waiting for him, grinning at him, were the two men in brown!

Came a second gust of wind. Which performed a curious office. Or it might have been the effect of the amazed and horrified child's scream . . . for sudden noises of a certain pitch, sometimes have the power of a giant's hand.

A quantity of snow shook and fell from the mechanism of the windmill: which now began to turn. And draw up the air into the shaft, thus setting into motion all the stagnant, thick, and heavy vapors that lay in the deep, stone veins of the Jail. Up they came, blundering into the churning mill. But this was not all. A second, more fearful circumstance attended. An uproar—as if the lid of Hell itself had been lifted—filled the shaft and shrieked and jabbered to the sky!

Together with the air, there had been sucked up from the gratings—through every portage and vent—the furious and savage voices of the Jail's inhabitants! Groans from the Pressroom, curses from the Stone Hall, hard, high laughter from the Master Debtors, and shrieks and wild whisperings from holds and wards and cells unknown —all mingled together in a chorus of truly monstrous scope and dimension!

Fearfully, the men in brown stared to one another! Till they recalled their purpose. They looked down. Then added their own curses to the dreadful torrent! The boy was gone!

Smith, choked, deafened, and despairing, had let go his hold. Eight feet he'd thumped—to the bottom of the shaft.

Then, his force not spent, he'd slipped, squealing, down a hole of formidable steepness—a vent that led, God knew where!

Had Smith been brought up to the Church, he'd have had a prayer off pat, for he traveled at speed on what he was sure was his last journey. (But, if he'd been brought up to the Church, he'd most likely not have been falling down a ventilator in Newgate Jail!)

"Gawd!" he panted. "Watch out—for 'ere comes Smith!"

And then—from some seven feet above the floor, between the pulpit and the open pews of the prison chapel— shot out a dusty, dirty bundle of commotion that howled as it fell, picked itself up—and bolted directly for the door!

Smith was back in jail.

The chapel was empty: but outside of its door was a regular hubbub. The last sermon had just been preached over Dick Mulrone. He was on his way to the hangman's cart. All of his friends, all of his admirers, all of his well- wishers had come to watch him—and now crowded the passages for a last pat on the back and a last sad wave.

The crowd was terrrific—more than enough to engulf the scurrying Smith. On all fours he went, among skirts and legs that were like a trampling forest.

"Got to get out! Got to get out!" he muttered—and butted and bit his way along. He came to a corner at the head of some stairs, was momentarily free—

"Smut!" shrieked a voice. "It's Smut!"

His sisters! Come to attend his trial: but first had been dragged by Lord Tom to see the last of the hero of Houns- low Heath. ("Give him a good send-off, m'dears! He'd have done as much for me!")

"Got to get out!" panted Smith, still on his hands and

knees and glaring up at his family like he was their faithful
mongrel hound.

"Oh Smut!" cried Miss Fanny. "You'll be took and
ironed for this!"

"Quick!" whispered Miss Bridget, handsome in her
Tuesday best. "Under my skirt, child! Pop underneath—
and not a sound!"

Miss Bridget tipped her great hoop so's her skirt rose
like a monstrous black bell about to chime against the
strongly pantalooned clappers which were her legs. Smith
looked briefly at his elder sister—and grinned. He darted
forward—and Miss Bridget dropped her skirt!

So began Smith's escape from Newgate Jail: not at all
as he'd dreamed—and certainly not as had been planned
for him . . . but rather a quiet, muffled exit through the
great Gate itself.

True, there were alarms on the way: and some discom-
forts. Smith found it hard to keep out of the way of Miss
Bridget's feet, else she found it hard to prevent herself
booting her felonious brother as if for his sins.

Miss Fanny also gave cause for alarm by asking aloud
if, "little Smut was all right in his flannel nest?" Till Miss
Bridget was heard to declare aloud that:

"You are a foolish cow, Fan! Hold your tongue, for
Pity's sake!"

Then Lord Tom joined them (Smith would have known
those sturdy feet anywhere!) and Miss Fanny couldn't
resist whispering:

"We've got him safe and sound! You'll never guess
where, Lord Tom! Not in a thousand years!"

But it seemed Miss Fanny ogled and stared and giggled
so much at her sister's heaving skirt that Lord Tom
guessed directly; but he had the good sense to hold his

peace and bid Miss Fanny to do likewise.

Then, at last, they were outside and beginning to walk away.

"Look! Look!" shrieked Miss Fanny, suddenly. "Oh Brid! Look!"

She pointed. Miss Bridget paled. Lord Tom looked alarmed.

In the thick snow behind Miss Bridget were not only her own footprints but the unmistakeable hop and scamper marks of an extra pair of feet!

"We'll walk behind you, Brid," said Miss Fanny—and for the rest of that extraordinary journey Miss Bridget had two of the most particular and devoted followers a lady could have wished for. They followed in all of her four footprints with a caution and respect most exemplary!

By the time they got to Turnmill Street, it was hard on ten o'clock.

"Home, child!" whispered Miss Bridget—and raised her skirt a trifle to step across the familiar door of the "Red Lion Tavern." And as she did so, there was a faint shouting and roaring that seemed to be coming from a long way off.

"What was that, Lord Tom?"

The highwayman sighed.

"From Tyburn, m'dear. They've just nubbed grand Dick Mulrone! I'm the only one left, Fanny. When will it be my turn?"

IF EVER A MAN could tell, to the nearest five minutes, how long it would take a particular coach leaving a particular part of the Town and going North, to come to the edge of the Finchley Common, that man was Lord Tom. Not your fat rumbling trundler nor your light-slung gig—passing northward through the Town—was capable of keeping Lord Tom waiting upon his wild and lonely hunting ground. He knew their paces as well as his own and boasted famously that his prizes came, so to speak, by prompt appointment.

Indeed, it was said in the trade, that Lord Tom might have made a better living by employing his genius in Town and auctioning his judgment for others to ride out for the "stand and deliver." Not that he didn't ride well and shoot well, but it was sometimes said (by those who'd accompanied him) that his nature was too bold for so secret an undertaking—and he was inclined to show courage when there was no call for it.

"Given the size of the coach as you've described it, given this weather, given the crowds for Dick Mulrone, given the starting from Vine Street—your Mister Mansfield will take luncheon at the 'Queen's Head' in Lamb's Conduit Fields and come upon the Common at half after four o'clock. 'Tis certain, Smut. Sure as we're in this cellar. Sure as my name's Lord Tom. At half after four. And at five—" He paused, his finger raised, like he was hailing a chair.

"At five, Lord Tom?"

"We'll have him!" (Sharp as a shot.)

Miss Fanny looked at her friend admiringly, but Smith was yet doubtful.

"Ye-es, Lord Tom . . . if *someone else* don't 'ave him first!" Lord Tom sighed and scratched his cheek, then examined the hand he'd employed.

"D'you mean our two friends in brown?"

Smith shivered—and nodded.

Said Miss Fanny, "Lord Tom'll see them off, Smut! You'll see!"

And Lord Tom, with a mighty scowl, agreed.

"I'll blow blue daylight through 'em, Smut! There's never a man yet who's dared come 'tween Lord Tom and his lawful prize! You'll see 'em scamper, my lad!"

"And then—our dockiment, at last!"

"The document!" suddenly exclaimed Miss Bridget, bitterly. For all this while, during the making and testing of the plan, she'd kept a resentful quiet; but now she could no more hold her peace.

"How I hate and despise it! For it's brought an old man to his death and made murderers of nought but common thieves! And now—and now it's turned our own poor mite (what has never sinned deeper than a passing pocket) into a dwarfish toby! To take such a child onto the murdering Common for to rob a blind man! Oh for shame-shame-shame!"

Lord Tom chewed his lip and shook his head. He stood up with a clatter of ironware and began to pace such of the cellar as admitted him.

"What would you have me do, Miss Bridget? In your own very hearing—not an hour ago, in this very residence —I've a-pleaded with him: I've a-begged him: I've a-warned him and I've a-supplicated with him not to come! But that lad's determined. Nothing anyone can say will shake him. He's iron, Miss Bridget. He's steel. He's rock. He's a fixture, ma'am!"

Smith—who felt as far from any of these things as was imaginable—nodded vigorously.

Since he'd left the dreadful Jail—even in the vinegary, rustling blackness of his sister's skirt, with her legs coming and going like engines of destruction—he'd thought of nothing but Mr. Mansfield with the fatal document on his way to Prickler's Hill. To say that nothing would have stopped Smith wasn't quite true. A knife in the ribs would have stopped him; likewise, a ball in the chest. But Lord Tom's warnings and Miss Bridget's respectable anger stood but a small chance against the furious urgings of his own heart and head.

Miss Fanny—to do her justice—must have seen this right from the start, for she never opposed her "sweet Smut" but agreed, "our dockiment must come first." Miss Bridget upbraided her, sneered at her, called her an "avaricious slut." But Miss Fanny only looked forgiving as her

sister railed, put her arm 'round Smith's shoulders and declared: "If his heart's in it, Brid, dear—'tis wicked to
thwart him!"

So Miss Bridget turned the full force of her tongue
upon Lord Tom who was somewhat shaken by it: for he
had, maybe, more prideful feelings than had Miss Fanny.
So the highwayman was driven to defend himself and feel
that he had to restore himself in Miss Fanny's and Smith's
eyes.

Not that Miss Bridget's tempest could ever have sunk
Lord Tom in Smith's bright eyes . . . for the boy ever held
the green-cloaked robber in the deepest admiration and
respect. Which respect, agreeable enough, was treasured
up by Lord Tom as a bright warm day to remember in the
too-soon close winter of his life. With energy and dignity,
he painted such a picture of his trade that only the coldest
of hearts could have scorned.

"Gallantry, ma'am, there's gallantry on the Common!
And fierce beauty and soaring adventure!"

The highwayman's eyes sparkled, and he brushed the
back of his hand across his cheek as if he could feel the
wild night upon it. Then he went on to relate exploits that
he'd told of many times before—but never so handsomely.
And he spoke of other famous gentlemen who'd once
waited, hid, and pounced where *he* now waited, hid, and
pounced. Duval—("Hanged!" snapped Miss Bridget.)
Turpin—("Hanged!")—Captain Robinson ("Hanged!").

"Yes, ma'am, they paid for their joys! They're dead
and gone . . . and so's a great many other folk. 'Tis
the common penalty for living. But it's not the quiet,
mewing, moaning bed-perishings that haunt the Common
of a moony night. No, ma'am! When we ride out, we
ride with the great ghostly company of the nubbed! Many
a time I've heard, 'Lord Tom, Lord Tom—I'm a-watching

you, friend!' in Turpin's own voice!"

Then Lord Tom, with dreamy grandeur, told of these dead men's doings in the days of their lives—and then of his own (to draw a parallel)—then back again . . . till it was hard to tell who'd done what: Duval, Robinson, Turpin—or Lord Tom.

In spite of herself, Miss Bridget's heart beat a little faster for she was but three and twenty and Miss Fanny's and Smith's sister, when all was said and done.

Smith's heart, also, was beating faster—but from a strong anxiety that Lord Tom's eloquence was dangerously delaying them, and that they'd be too late upon the Common. For the first time in his life he wished Lord Tom had had fewer adventures—and hadn't remembered them so well! In his fearful mind's eye he saw the two men in brown and, maybe, the lurking shadow of Mr. Green, waiting for a certain well-remembered coach . . . He saw the gleam of a knife and heard a breathlessly whispered: "And good day to you, you blind old fool!"

"By tonight we'll have our dockiment safe and sound," he heard Miss Fanny murmur. "And Smut'll read it to us . . . with new tallows and we three sat at the table . . . for all the world, Brid, like reading a psalm from the Scriptures."

The document! With a start, Smith remembered it. Not that he'd ever forgot it, but its importance now seemed changed. If, by destroying the document, he could have destroyed Mr. Green and his friends, he'd have done so. For the document was now not so much a means of his going up in the world, but a way of preventing his going down...

"Well, Smut, me comrade-in-arms of this day! Are we fit and ready?" exclaimed Lord Tom at last, staring at a fine French watch that had been the subject of his last-told adventure ('A duke's, no less!'). "Five minutes to make your adieus, Smut—then it's the Common for the pair of us!"

Thankfully, and with mounting excitement, Smith left his seat and stationed himself beside the tremendous highwayman when Miss Bridget, somewhat desperately, protested:

"But he'll freeze to death! He cannot go so ill-dressed!"

A further delay, while an ancient cloak was found to cover Smith's draggled finery, and a queer hat (that Miss Fanny had once toyed with), to cover his tangled and matted head. He had a certain shabby splendor, and even Miss Bridget gazed at him with surprise and a certain reluctant admiration as he began to mount the stairs. And Smith, caught full in the romantic spirit, felt himself full of the gallantest dreams. He turned, waved and cried:

"Adieu, dear ladies! Wish me—"

He stopped. There was a loud knock on the door!

"Gawd!" muttered Smith (with an alley's length of curses in addition), "it's for me!"

He bolted back into the cellar, his cloak flapping like ruined wings, and hid behind the curtain. Lord Tom stood, grandly guarding his small friend's sanctuary: and the two sisters rose together.

"Come in!"

Enter a small, wizened man with eager eyes and a bundle. He peered down into the body of the cellar and grinned and nodded to the company. Mr. Jones's assistant. Not for Smith: but with Dick Mulrone's fine suit. To be altered. Who for? Ha-ha! You'd never guess! Mister Jones's father! There's a good son for you!

He threw the bundle on the table and said Mr. Jones himself would be calling to describe his father's figure and shape. Tomorrow. Today he was tired out. The crowds! The shouting! Fairly frayed him!

Then he went—and left behind a gloomy silence. If ever four souls and a cellar were haunted by the lack of a ghost, they were gathered now. A coat, a waistcoat—and a pair of breeches. That was all there was of Dick Mulrone. No breath nor whisper of a ghost came into the "Red Lion's" cellar to quicken the four sad hearts or stir the pitiful heap of clothing. The gallantest robber of the Hounslow Heath was as dead as mutton; not able, even, to haunt his own breeches.

Lord Tom bowed his head. Miss Fanny wept. Said Miss Bridget, "Take care of him, Lord Tom. For my heart chills. Watch over little Smut."

"I'll guard him, ma'am. With me very life! I do assure you, while he's with Lord Tom no danger will offer. I—I promise you, ma'am! Come, lad—away!"

With the best will in the world, Lord Tom tried to be in good spirits on the way to Finchley Common, but the sadness lingered, and he kept falling into a silence as heavy as the glum sky. And Smith, whose dearest dream and brightest hope had come to pass: viz. that he should be riding out with his hero, Lord Tom, for to go on the snaffling lay, was as melancholy as sin. Sitting on the front of the highwayman's saddle, he turned round from time to and saw Lord Tom's great, bristling face, dark under his hat, much troubled . . .

So they rode on, this weirdly romantic and strongly fantastic pair—the infant jailbird and the glowering highwayman—through the thick snow that lay and tumbled, toward the famous place where Lord Tom and all of his hanged ghosts, waited, hid—and pounced.

THE SNOW, which had held off for some three hours, began again in earnest at about four o'clock, when the light was perishing from the sky and there came up to "Bob Bellamy's Inn" on the steep of Highgate Hill a most weary horse bearing a full-sized man and an undersized boy.

"Is this the place, Lord Tom?"

"The very same."

"Bob Bellamy's Inn," a pleasant, new-built structure with three parlors and rooms for seven gentlemen (three double and one single), sat about fifty yards northward from the top of Highgate Hill and commanded a spacious view of the southern fingers of Finchley Common, from which it was distant by about half a steep mile. Thus from the snug windows not a curricle, gig, or coach could venture onto the Common without being interestedly viewed. And, for the further entertainment of his customers, Mr. Bellamy had provided a strong spyglass (at sixpence for the half-hour) and certain information that might be of service. For Mr. Bellamy's customers were high tobies to a man.

"Knew 'em all!" was Mr. Bellamy's proud boast as he stood by the cheerful fire of an evening. "Duval—Turpin —Robinson . . . Many's the time they've sat about this very snug, drinking and laughing—and popping to the windows for a nifty look!" (This, notwithstanding the glum fact that Duval had been hanged eighty years before, and Bob Bellamy looked no more than forty.) "Yes, indeed! Knew 'em all!"

He welcomed Lord Tom and grinned affectionately at Smith, whom he recognized as a "brisk, bright, and prosperous apprentice to the Trade." He made a place for the highwayman and his apprentice by the fire and despatched an evil-eyed potboy for "jars of the best."

"Nothing coming, nothing going," he murmured, jerking his head to the windows that commanded the best view of the Common. "Not our sort of weather, eh, Lord Tom? Many's the time—ah! many's the time great Duval himself would curse the snow for muffling his pickings! Aye! And a-warming his glorious backside where you're a-warming yours, friend!"

For Lord Tom was handsomely thawing himself out, and fizzing and drizzling into the hearth. His caped coat, whited like a sepulcher, was now beginning to patch through into a wet green—like a lawn after winter. Likewise, Smith, buffeted and stung by the whirling snow, bruised beyond belief by the dreadful horse, began to come to himself and crack and thaw and ease himself into a furtive smile.

"There's a coach due, Bob, within—" (Lord Tom drew out his French watch which the landlord eyed merrily and murmured, "Ah! we remember that one, eh?") "—within this half-hour. From Town toward Barnet."

"You know best, friend. You got a reputation. But it surprises me: yes, indeed. Must be powerful business to draw an equipage across this murderous white nothingness!"

"It is, Bob. It surely is."

He winked at Smith—then raised his fingers warningly to his lips as the potboy returned with the ale.

Not fifty yards to the west of "Bob Bellamy's" stood another inn—an ancient, tottery, smoky building, the speaking likeness of Smith's "Red Lion." This was "The Wrestlers." It seemed that Lord Tom had a little brief business there. He charged Smith to wait for him: not to stir from Mr. Bellamy's parlor: under no circumstances.

Mr. Bellamy nodded. Lord Tom wasn't to worry. His own stout person would go bail for the apprentice's not shifting. Not till Lord Tom returned. The highwayman thanked him, then turned to his apprentice:

"So watch out for the coach, Smut. Mister Bellamy'll show you where. Here's a sixpence, Bob! Let the lad watch through the spyglass! Let him be a real high toby while I'm gone! Just for ten minutes, eh?"

He tossed a coin on the table, but Bob Bellamy shook his greasy, good-natured head.

"Keep your money, friend! On a night like this, I'm all for the warmth of kindness. The lad can watch for free! Duval would have liked that! Yes, sir! I can hear him say,

'Bob! Let the lad watch for free!' "

"There, Smut," said Lord Tom, with sudden pride. "There's a small taste of our companionage! You're among friends!"

Then, with a quick wave, he opened the door, his place was took by a flurry of snow, and he was striding across the invisible road to "The Wrestlers."

"A grand fellow!" remarked Bob Bellamy. "One of the best!"

He eased himself into a seat close by Smith and prepared to unburden himself of all his superior memories for the amazement of a new pair of ears. But Smith was staring so fiercely and anxiously at the window that overlooked the approaches to the Common, that Bob Bellamy (seeing his best tales might pass unheeded) took pity on the boy and pointed to where the spyglass stood on the mantel-shelf.

"Take it, lad. Go watch for the coach. And remember, through that selfsame glass the proudest, sharpest, gallantest eyes these parts have ever known, once stared. May their brilliance lighten your viewing. Go stand by the window . . . elbows on the sill . . . left knee cocked on the seat. The very attitude of Turpin! Duval was a taller man. He always used to sit . . ."

The capacious-memoried landlord rambled on, following Smith from the fire to the window, obliging him by pulling out the spyglass into all of its gilt sections—then standing to one side with the warming remark that Smith was "the very image of Claude Duval as a lad!"

Smith, pleased in spite of his urgency, stared out into the gathering night: past the ghostly reflection of his own thin, fierce face, through the snow-filled air, onto the deep white world that sank and humped and valleyed and hillocked for many a quiet, mysterious mile. This was northward. Southward lay the Town, speckled and spotted with lights . . .

"D'you see that long shadowy finger?" breathed Bob Bellamy. "That's the road the coach'll come by . . . *if* it comes."

Smith saw, and raised the spyglass so's the landscape jumped amazingly close at hand. He saw bushes and trees creaking under their white fruit, which, every once in a while, the wind would shift and cause to thump and shower down, adding more whiteness to the overburdened ground.

And then, distant even in the spyglass, he saw a square black creature, with a pair of gleaming yellow eyes, tipping and lumbering in the wake of two horses—as if it would catch them if it could, but was yet in danger of giving up the struggle and perishing in the cold.

"It's coming!" muttered Smith, triumphantly. "Lord Tom had best be quick!"

He turned to the side window and swung the spyglass toward "The Wrestlers," to see if the romantic figure of the highwayman was yet come out and was leaning through the whirling weather . . .

Amazing! So strong was the glass that Smith felt he could have touched the door and walls! And poked his head through the parlor window (for, like "Bob Bellamy's," "The Wrestlers" had good spying windows, well eaved against the weather) to say: "Make haste, Lord Tom! The coach is sighted! Hurry, good friend of mine! Get up off your chair! Hurry! Leave those—"

Those what? For there sat Lord Tom, large and near as life, leaning across a table—in a deep discussion with . . .

Smith wiped the spyglass for a sudden flux of sweat had

misted it. He looked again. He grew vastly pale. He began to tremble. His skin began to prickle as if the air was full of thorns and arrows. His belly turned unquiet and he would be sick.

Lord Tom was in deep discussion with the two men in brown! Lord Tom. His strong friend, his champion, even his hero . . . Very fearful of face was he: very cringing, very humble—"Yes, sirs! No, sirs! The boy's as good as dead, sirs! Aye—and the blind man, too! Ain't I betrayed the lad neatly? Hope you're pleased with me, sirs!"

Smith put down the glass.

"What's amiss, lad?"

"Nothing! You mind your own damned business, Mister Bellamy—and I'll mind mine!"

Not very distinct. Smith spoke through his hands—which were before his face to hide his rushing tears! A very black, bitter, and tragical place was the world to Smith as he understood the scope of his friend's treachery. Not Miss Fanny's prattling had betrayed his whereabouts always but the whispers of gallant Lord Tom! The blind man's turning against him was as nothing to the wretchedness he now endured. For Smith had been struck deep indeed . . .

"I'll fetch you a tot of brandy, lad!" murmured Bob Bellamy, much concerned and believing the apprentice to be, so to speak, the victim of "stagecoach fright." "That'll put fire into you for the 'stand and deliver'!"

He was gone but a second, he swore—no more: but when he returned the door was banging open and the parlor was empty, save for a ghost in the snow! The highwayman's apprentice was gone!

"Come back! Come back!" he bellowed—but the small, tumbling, hurtling figure that plunged down the hillside was fast vanishing and heeded him not.

In places the snow law two feet deep and Smith, to rise out of it, had to bound in a mighty, springing fashion—like a tremendous flea. But every now and then he'd strike on an unexpectedly shallow patch, so his feet, meeting resistance, would shoot him more powerfully than ever into the air—from which he'd fall and roll over and over in a whirl of white. Then up he'd scramble, wet and panting, to bound onward—till he fell again . . .

Such tracks as he made were almost instantly filled in after him so that the effect of his progress was oddly supernatural. And all the while, in a harshly sobbing voice, he'd plead and cajole and beg and curse and revile and threaten his own despairing person to hurry, hurry, hurry!

Three devils were after him: two in brown—and one in green! But the snow kept flinging coldly suffocating arms about him—as if to hold him forever in its freezing bosom: and as he rose the very heavens seemed to beat him down again with their fluffy torrents. The whole huge Universe was turned against him: the earth, the sky, the wind—and even his own failing limbs which ached for nothing more than a bed in the dreadful, loving snow.

But each time, there came up out of the hole he'd made in the ground, a small rebellious voice:

"Come on with you, Smith! You dozy weasel! Up! Up! What for did you come out of the 'ouse of bondage? To sink and perish in this great Fleet Ditch of common 'opelessness? Not bleeding likely!" And then, in tones which shook with bitterness, grief, and contempt: "So to 'ell with you, Lord Tom! For that's where you belongs!"

On which the indomitable figure of Smith would rise up out of the white, and fumble on.

Where to? To the road the coach would take. But where was it? He stared about him. Whiteness everywhere. No landmark, no post—nothing at all!

Once more, a feeling of hopelessness gripped him. He looked back up the hill. Three small black figures were on their way—murder in their every motion! So where was the road vanished to? Was even that against him? In a sudden rage, Smith stamped his foot and glared about him—

Not seventy yards off lumbered the coach! Toward him! The road—he was on it!

The horses panted and dragged and steamed. The coachman, high up on his snowcapped black mountain, leaned forward, eyes fairly glued to the vague shadow which was all he could see of firm ground. He dared not look elsewhere for one false move might end in a drift . . . and finish the vital journey then and there.

Smith scrambled aside: sank up to his knees in snow. Crouched down. Wished to God he'd waited for Bob Bellamy's tot of brandy: for what parts of him the weather neglected to chill, fright did for wonderfully.

On came the coach, its yellow lamps leaping like alarmed eyes as it rocked perilously. All haste and commotion—yet soundless. The snow and the wind muffled all. Might have been a spectral equipage; already lost some way back, and only its spirit persisting . . .

Now it was close enough for Smith to pick out the coachman's features: his one-time master in the Vine Street yard. He heard the horses thumping in the snow, and the harness groan and creak in the angry singing of the air. Still he waited. The coach drew level—

A friendly gust of wind whipped and whirled and sent stinging flakes into the coachman's face and eyes. Smith shifted. Vastly quick. He seized hold on the door. Dragged it open—

"Who's there? Who is it?"

Mr. Mansfield's voice, angry and alarmed, was swallowed up in the wind.

Smith reached within. Clutched at a coat sleeve—a wrist—a hand. Pulled with all his might!

"My God! My God!"

Out heaved the blind man, falling with the tilt of the coach, out into the muffling snow!

"For God's sake, who is it? What d'you want with me?"

Smith, still holding tight, answered nothing. Instead, he dragged him down into the drifts by the side of the road while the untenanted coach—its door swinging helpless, like a one-armed soldier's sleeve—quaked and jolted unknowing, on . . .

Again the blind man cried out, and Smith fixed his hand over the betraying mouth and, in a whisper no man could have recognized, breathed:

"Quiet—if you values yore life!"

Twenty yards on, the coach rocked to a halt. It had been accosted. Pistols pointed the way to the coachman's brains. Which were spinning with anxiety.

The wind whipped familiar voices back to where the snow was fast hiding Smith and his prisoner.

"The lousy coach is empty!"

"Thank the Lord!" (The coachman)

"That boy of your'n—Lord-piddling-Tom! He's beat us to it!"

"Friends!" (Lord-piddling-Tom) "I swear I did what I could."

"Not enough, not enough! You should have slit his mean throat—you green windbag!"

"Friends, friends! How was I to know . . ."

"You swore you'd fix him!"

"And so I meant to! I swear it!"

"Swear it to Mister Green! If he gives you leave! You'll bleed for this!"

"No! No! They must be near at hand! Let's search!"

"In this great 'owling blizzard?"

"Yes-yes!"

"We've 'ad experience afore! Your little rat near killed us once with chasing him!" (Smith, in concealment, couldn't restrain a beam of pride.)

"Then what's to be done?"

"On to Mister Green in the morning. That's what."

"But-but—"

" 'But' to yore heart's content, fat man. Yore day's done. You blotted yore book. Maybe with blood, eh?"

"The coach! The coach!"

While they'd been thus engaged the coachman had took advantage. He'd whipped his horses and yelled them into a frenzy. Already, the coach heaved and plunged on its way!

"Stop, you fool! Stop—or you're dead!"

Lord Tom raised his pistol—aimed—and fired! A cry from ahead. The coachman, high up, clutched at his side and began to slip . . . then seemed to recover himself partly . . . then was lost from sight behind a clump of trees. When the coach reappeared, still lumbering fast, there was nothing on the box but a heavy, jerking shape that, any moment, would fall by the wayside, unheeded . . .

Smith, in his excitement, had withdrawn his hand from the magistrate's mouth.

"Is he—is he—killed?" whispered Mr. Mansfield.

Smith did not answer. Instead, with bitter, lonely eyes, he watched the three figures turn and begin their climb up the hill. Then he stood up, brushed the accumulated snow from the magistrate's shoulders and head, and pulled him to his feet.

Four miles to the North lay Prickler's Hill. Smith set his face in that direction and, with his hand firmly about the blind man's wrist, began to walk. And the snow came down like a disaster . . .

chapter SIXTEEN

THEY MADE poor progress. In two hours something less than three quarters of a mile. No more. Every once in a while, the boy would turn his back to the weather and face the blind man, drawing him on and, at the same time, seeming to retreat under the impassive stare of the snow-stained face. For there was no doubt the blind man sensed the scrutiny of unseen eyes (or did he feel warm breath softening the bitter wind?) and, as was his old habit, emptied his face of all telltale expression . . . Then the boy would grunt and turn about—to plod on in the scourging snow.

Sometimes, when they passed among the heavily band-aged trees, the wind would dislodge snow from the lower branches so's it thumped down, knocking the breath out of the two travelers and forcing them to halt for recovery. Then the blind man would once more ask his guide who he was and why he'd saved him and was leading him through this huge and bitter night. Perhaps he knew? Hard to say.

"Very well, then—speak . . . anything . . . anything at all. Or are you dumb? A fine pair, we two! One with no tongue to tell what he sees, and the other with no eyes to see what's worth the telling. A humorous pair! Well, then —if you won't speak, sing!"

But Smith uttered never a word. Why? He was deeply frightened of the magistrate's mania for justice. He dreaded the blind man would give him up at the first opportunity. "So let 'im think it's a perishing angel what's leading 'im!" thought Smith cunningly: and held his tongue.

At about seven o'clock the snow began to abate— though the wind did not—and a great clearness and brilliancy settled upon the landscape, across which the boy and the blind man seemed to be the only moving things.

The magistrate, having worn out his conversation, turned to singing and chanting (maybe in the hope his silent guide would join in and betray himself?).

"The Lord is my shepherd, I shall not want." ("You said it!" thought Smith, plodding on.)

"He maketh me to lie down in green pastures . . ." ("You should see 'em," mouthed Smith with fierce irony.)

"Oh you should see 'em!" He blinked about him where the hills were white and the valleys were white: likewise the slopes between. The sky alone offered relief, being of a velvety blackness, pricked out with some fifteen or twenty frosty stars.

"Thou preparest a table before me in the presence of mine enemies . . ." went on the blind man: and Smith scowled through his windy tears, for he'd not eaten that day . . .

The thought struck him that Mr. Mansfield knew who he was all the time and was subtly mocking him—till the chance should offer of giving him up. Certainly, everything the blind man said seemed now to be cruelly humorous: and he said a great deal! Songs and poems and lumps of the Scriptures came puffing out his mouth with much issuage of smoking breath. For this was Mr. Mansfield's stock-in-trade, his vision of the world, seen through other men's eyes who'd digested their vision into words: and it made him a supper for to last him all of his life.

His own memories of what the world looked like he no longer trusted. He was a sensible man and knew full well the changes that must have been wrought since last he'd looked. His beloved daughter could no longer have been the fearful child caught in the fire he'd remembered for so long. Even the Town itself he knew to be much changed, for everywhere he heard sounds of building and of tumbling and of men losing their way. Even Nature herself he suspected of ageing—and the wind and the cold seemed crueller than he recalled.

Maybe, they were even breeding a new style of boy, now? He smiled—or tried to, but his cheeks were partly frozen. The child, Smith, for instance . . . He frowned as he recalled the powerful evidence against him. No. Whatever else might alter, justice remained fixed—like God Himself. Justice: the last refuge of a blind man.

Suddenly, he felt the grip on his wrist disappear! Frightened, he stopped—turned his face this way and that in the lonely wind. Had he been left? Oh God! Why?

Smith, beaten breathless by the weather, with a lock of his black hair (his hat was in "Bob Bellamy's") frozen solid so's it banged against his forehead like a door-knocker, was suddenly attacked by commonsense. The old mole-in-the-hole was not changed. Stern and cold was his face, colder even than the snow that spotted it. Smith was not leading him, but he was leading Smith: back into the horrible house of bondage! A thousand windy voices shouted in his ears, bidding him leave the old Justice and be gone! The world was a freezing, lonely place. No one would give Smith quarter in it. Not his sisters, not his treacherous friend—and, least of all, the stern-faced magistrate. Not even the howling weather!

Further and further off backed Smith, amazed by his own madness in coming thus far. He stared at the stark, menacing form of the blind man with his stony heart. "Take, take, take! And never give nought in return! I'm done with you!"

And then, as Smith watched, the blind man raised his hands. He turned about: tried to take a step: stumbled: recovered himself—and cried out:

"Am I alone? Am I alone?"

His face, though much limited in expression by his shrouded eyes, was suddenly and deeply wretched. A desolate face, bespeaking a starved soul. For that soul of his had been nourished on thin fare these past twelve years: it had grown weak without his knowing it so that, when the wind blew, it bowed as if to break. And the wind blew as hard for the blind man as it did for the boy.

"You old blind Justice, you!" mumbled Smith lurching back to Mr. Mansfield. "Give us your hand, then!"

The magistrate stretched out his hands—and Nature made strange amends for a certain disability of his. Snow, dislodged from his spectacles and fallen again his eyes, had begun to melt. Water trickled down his cheeks as if it was doing what he could not: weeping.

Bewildered, Smith gazed on Mr. Mansfield's melting face. He took both the oustretched hands.

" 'ere—'ere, then! Both me hands! You ain't alone, Mister Mansfield—nor never was! I—I was only resting."

"Smith-Smith-Smith!" cried the blind man, grasping in return the hands he'd never forgot. "Your voice at last! How I longed to hear it!"

"You knew it was me, then?"

"Yes, yes!"

"Then—why didn't you say?"

"You didn't want me to know, did you?"

"No. I was thinking you'd 'and me over to the law."

"And even so you came back?"

"I'm only a 'uman bein'."

"Only!"

Smith freed one of Mr. Mansfield's hands and turned once more into the weather.

"We'd best be moving—or we'll freeze in situation!"

They stumbled on a while longer, but no more in silence. A curious warmth seemed to've sprung up between them and rendered the wind less savage. Mr. Mansfield told Smith that his daughter had stayed behind to attend his trial and, maybe, to keep Mr. Billing to his promise of the adjournment. It seemed she, the "Saint of Vine Street," had kept her faith in Smith.

"Not you, Mister Mansfield?" asked Smith, wistfully.

"No, alas, not me. I'm no saint, Smith. Like you, I'm only a human being."

"Queer, then, being an old mole-in-the-hole and 'elp-less, you should come out in sich weather for . . . for what,

Mister Mansfield? For the 'ealthy cold air?"

Mr. Mansfield grinned awkwardly.

"That's it, Smith! For my health!"

Smith grinned back—then remembered his companion's disability and said:

"I'm a-smiling, Mister Mansfield!"

"Pleased to hear it, Smith."

"You, too, Mister Mansfield. And a very cheering thing to see. You got a friendly smile, you know."

"I didn't know, Smith. But now you've mentioned it, I'll take a special pride in it!"

And Mr. Mansfield continued to smile into the icy wind in the firm hope that Smith would sometimes turn and get the benefit. Which Smith did, and always remembered to return the compliment aloud. Then he'd turn back again and chatter about what he could see and what he'd seen . . . describing his life and the doings of his sisters . . . and even his escape from Newgate Jail. But he never mentioned Lord Tom nor any of the darkness that hemmed him in. Likewise, with Mr. Mansfield. Though he confided in Smith much of his warmer past, he, too, said nothing of what must have lain deepest in both their thoughts: viz. the murder of Mr. Field.

Presently, they reached the top of a gentle slope.

"Cottage, Mister Mansfield. Quarter mile off. Light in the window. Nice, snug little place. Looks warm. What say we knock on the door?"

"Don't mind if we do."

So Smith tucked his head as far as it would go into his collar, and began the descent toward the cottage which lay in a snow-filled hollow.

A neat, well-built cottage with good windows and a stout

fence marking off its garden from the Common—though with the snow lying so heavy on garden and Common alike, the fence looked more peevish than necessary. But there was so strong a blossoming of smoke from the chimney that it bespoke a warmer nature within than without . . . and the cottage's eyes gleamed most cheerfully.

All this Smith described to Mr. Mansfield, who nodded as they approached the door and said he was reminded of old fairy tales.

"A wood chopper's cottage, an old wood chopper and his brown-eyed wife."

"Then there's money in chopping wood," said Smith, shrewdly, "for there's a stable at the back and space for a carriage."

He knocked on the door and Mr. Mansfield sighed as if he was almost sorry that their winter's journey—murderous as it had been—was ending in so ordinary and genteel a place. No wood chopper, no charcoal burner, no witch even . . .

The door opened: an inch.

"Who's there? What d'you want?" (The voice was harsh—even irritable.)

"Shelter!" cried Smith and Mr. Mansfield together.

"Who for?"

"A blind man and a froze child!"

"What was that?" (A woman's voice from within. Peevish.)

"Blind man and froze child," answered the first voice.

"Stuff and nonsense, Charlie!"

"That's what they said."

"Have a look!"

The door opened further . . . to the full extent of its

chain. A stout, waistcoated man, bald and frowning, peered out.

"Man and child, right enough, Mrs. P.!" he called out.

"How big, Charlie?"

"Child's about—um—high as your chair and the man's —um—taller than me."

"Don't like it, Charlie."

"No more do I. Shall I shut 'em out, Mrs. P.?"

"Good God, sir!" exclaimed Mr. Mansfield. "In humanity's name! On such a night!"

"Did you hear that, Mrs. P.? The weather, y'know!"

"Mrs. P.!" shouted Smith. "We're froze near to death— and me friend's as blind as a post!"

"Charlie! See if he's blind!" (Mrs. P. Somewhat complainingly.)

Obligingly, Mr. Mansfield took off his spectacles and presented his face.

"Nasty," said Charlie. "Blind all right."

"Then let 'em in, Charlie!" cried Mrs. P. "Keeping a blind man and a froze child on your doorstep! Ain't you got no humanity, sir? Oh you're a weak vessel, Charlie Parkin!"

Thereupon, the chain was unfastened, the door opened wide, and Smith and Mr. Mansfield welcomed directly into the parlor.

"Hats! Coats! Boots!" shouted Mrs. P. "Quick, Charlie! Into the kitchen with 'em before we're drowned out again!"

"Least said, soonest mended!" said Charlie, collecting up those snowy articles which were already dripping fast in the great heat of the parlor.

He bustled out, and Mrs. P.—a small, very small woman

with sharp features and a blue cap—fixed Smith and Mr. Mansfield on either side of the neat fire. Indeed, everything about the parlor was neat: the cloth upon the table was neatly embroidered with neat little flowers, the plates upon that cloth were neat, and even the crumbs remaining on those plates had been neatly arranged, like soldiers drawn up for review.

"A very neat home," said Smith to Mr. Mansfield.

"You poor things!" said Mrs. P., busy by the sideboard with glasses and some warming spirits. "Lost your ways on the Common, I suppose?"

"Our coach was held up, ma'am," said Mr. Mansfield. "Highwaymen."

"Charlie!" shouted Mrs. P. "They was held up! Highwaymen!"

Instantly, Charlie reappeared with a pistol in his hand. His eyes were fiery. "Highwaymen? Where?"

"No, no! They" (she nodded to Smith and Mr. Mansfield) "was held up by highwaymen. Victims, Charlie. And come to us for succor."

"Oh!" said Charlie, putting up his weapon. "Them damned high tobies!"

"Fetch the book, Charlie."

Charlie nodded, vanished back into the kitchen, and reappeared with spectacles and a green ledger.

"Ink and a fresh pen, Charlie."

They were got from the sideboard.

"Brown paper, Charlie."

This was to spread on the tablecloth to protect it from the consequences of Charlie's writings.

"Now, Charlie—off you go!"

Wondering, Smith watched and Mr. Mansfield listened to these preparations.

"Blind man and boy," said Mrs. P.—and Charlie repeated it and slowly, with much help from his fumbling tongue, wrote it in the book.

"Held up—where was you held up?"

"On the Common, ma'am."

"On the Common, Charlie."

"On the Common, Mrs. P. Two m's and one n."

"Robbed?"

"No, ma'am."

"Not robbed, Charlie."

Charlie wrote and Mrs. P. sighed at her husband's slowness. ("A slow vessel, Mister Parkin.")

"Injured?"

"Our coachman was—murdered, I believe," said Mr. Mansfield, bitterly.

"Coachman murdered, Charlie."

Charlie looked up and exchanged a long, deep stare with Mrs. P. Then he shook his head. "Them damned high tobies!"

Now Mrs. P. came over with two glasses of spirits.

"Two measures of brandy, Charlie!" she called out as she offered them.

"Two measures of brandy," wrote Charlie. "And two suppers to follow, Mrs. P.?"

"Two suppers, Charlie—and two seats by the fire for the night." She turned to her guests.

"Nothing but chairs remaining."

Charlie finished his writing and looked up.

"Names? What names, please?"

"Mansfield," said the magistrate somewhat coolly, for he was more than surprised by the above formalities. "Mister Mansfield. Justice of the Peace, sir."

"A magistrate! Fancy that, Mrs. P.! Well, well, sir! It

seems we're in the same line of business, for I'm a constable—among other things. Yes, sir! Here to keep law and order! And let me tell you, sir, there's not a vagabond, rogue, or foot-pad who's dared set foot across the fence!"

"That's right!" agreed Mrs. P. "This cottage and all the ground enclosed by the fence belongs to the parish—and we keep it clean and aboveboard. The law's respected here, sir!"

"And everything's recorded," went on Charlie, patting the ledger. "Accounts square and trim. Two measures of brandy offered: two measures of brandy writ down: two measures of brandy back from the parish. Not a drop more, not a drop less."

"A name for honesty," said Mrs. P.

"And for neatness," added Charlie.

Smith looked at Mr. Mansfield, and observed his face had grown redder than the fire could have made it. For the magistrate felt that this demonstration of upholding the law struck too shrewdly to be smiled at. And maybe he wondered if the Parkins' neat cottage and clean garden, over which they watched so exactly—and let the rest of the Common go hang—was not an image of what his own heart had been . . . and, indeed, of the whole tidy business of the law itself.

Charlie had been about to put the ledger away, when a thought struck him.

"Lad's name, sir? Servant of your'n?"

"Friend!" said Mr. Mansfield, vigorously. "A friend!"

"Name?" said Charlie, his pen poised like a sword.

"Jones," lied Mr. Mansfield, blandly.

Smith, the escaped, and no doubt hunted jailbird, regarded the perjuring magistrate with the warmest affection. And surprise.

"Jones," wrote down Charlie, sanded the ink, and shut the ledger. He looked to Mrs. P.

"Shall we show why we got no bed to spare, Mrs. P.?"

"Parish business, Charlie. You ain't got the right."

"But he's a Justice, Mrs. P., and concerned, I fancy."

"You're a sentimental vessel, Charlie Parkin. Dangerous for one with your responsibilities."

"Just this once, Mrs. P. And he's blind."

"Very well, Charlie—as he's blind."

Whereupon the sentimental constable chuckled and reopened the ledger which he carried to Mr. Mansfield's side.

"There was someone before you, sir."

"Indeed?"

"We took him in."

"Generous, sir. Generous!"

"He was bleeding."

"Who was he?"

"Your coachman, sir. Yes, indeed—we've succoured him and nourished him and put him to bed."

"Thank God! Thank God!" cried Mr. Mansfield, deeply moved.

"Here it is," went on Charlie, proud to've been of service to humanity, the parish, *and* a justice of the peace. And forthwith, he read out the coachman's name, wound, where sustained, quantity of bandage applied, sustenance consumed, and quality of lodging, together with the care of horses and use of coach house. All of which was chargeable to the parish . . . as was the meager warmth from Charlie Parkin's respectable heart.

Then the ledger was put away and Mrs. P. busied herself with fetching hot suppers for her guests, while her husband talked and talked of how he kept his garden clear, and expressed the hope that Mr. Mansfield would bring his vigilance to the ears of all his legal friends in Town.

At about ten o'clock the Parkins went to bed (after assuring Mr. Mansfield that his coachman was not badly hurt and was sleeping peacefully) and left their guests to doze or brood in their chairs beside the banked-up fire.

"It's been a long day," murmured Mr. Mansfield.

"A long day," agreed Smith.

"A lifetime long."

Smith said nothing, but fancied he understood. Slowly, Mr. Mansfield's head sank down on his chest and his fine, strong face glowed in the firelight. Smith stared at him profoundly. Dreamily, he wondered what sort of man the magistrate had been before he'd lost his sight. He imagined him to've been . . .

"Smith!"

Mr. Mansfield was still awake. He'd taken off his spectacles and was staring to where he supposed Smith to be. His eyes were in a tragically ruinous state. But he was smiling. He fumbled inside his waistcoat.

"Here, Smith. Isn't this something you wanted? Take it then. Read it. Aloud, I beg of you!"

He was offering Smith the document!

THE DOCUMENT! All this time, in the snow when he and Mr. Mansfield had been alone, the precious item had been within his grasp—and he'd forgot it! Forgot it so entirely that its sudden appearance before the cottage fire was almost terrifying.

"Take it, Smith—and tell me what old Mister Field had to say."

Fearfully, Smith reached out his hand and took the document. Ten thousand thoughts, fears, and questions filled his head! Why had he been given it now? Why the enormous trust? For didn't the magistrate still believe him to be a murderer? Yet he trusted. But what other choice had he—in his condition? Trust was obligatory: a necessary quality of life.

"Read, Smith. Don't be afraid. Read!"

So Smith crouched down at the blind man's feet, close by the fire where the light was sufficient. And, as he sat, Mr. Mansfield's hand dropped by chance on his shoulder, then moved lightly upward and rested on his head.

Smith read: slowly, shakily—for he was not overly proficient, and the writing was crabbed, and there were words he could not pronounce . . .

Neither accusation, nor confession, nor deed to property was the document. It was a letter to Mr. Lennard. A strange letter of an uncanny power in the firelit room— for, as Smith read on, murdered old Mr. Field seemed to creep into the parlor and cast his cold shadow between the blind man and the boy, so that Mr. Mansfield shivered and withdrew his hand from Smith's head—and Smith shrank back toward his own side of the fire . . .

The old man had written in deep agitation. Something had disturbed and shaken him profoundly. Also, there was fear . . . of a distressing kind. He knew his life to be threatened. Several times, he mentioned it. "I lie awake of nights, Lennard, and hear such sounds, and have such thoughts . . . at my age!" Then, later, he wrote of a discovery he'd made—but did not say what . . . only that he meant to carry it to his grave. A terrible discovery. This, also, was repeated and underlined. "A *terrible, terrible* discovery."

But now came an oddity. An instruction quite plain and without any of the confused fears that invaded the rest of the document. "The trifle" ("Trifle" was underlined) "I wrote you of previously is buried in a shrewd place. Andrews knows where. Ask him where Jack used to play as a boy. When you have it, dispose of it as pleases you. I shall care no longer . . ." There followed here some bitter and pathetic words of the world in general, all once more in a very agitated manner, together with a last reference to his discovery, reaffirming his intention of carrying it to the grave, "where it will be hidden and forgot for ever."

Smith stopped reading. There was a restless silence in which the fire leaped and cast strange lightnings across the blind man's face.

"Go on," he said.

"There's nothing more."

"Nothing?"

"Nothing!" muttered Smith, bitterly. "Or d'you think I'm hiding the rest from you?"

He scowled furiously into the fire for his heart felt grievously empty. The document. The precious item that was to've raised him up in the world: nothing but an old man's misery and dread—and the whereabouts of a trifle . . . a locket, most likely, or a brooch with a twist of hair.

For this he'd endured so much. He stared at the paper, through which the fire shone redly, and noted the stains made by his own sweat when first he'd fled from the men in brown. Then he remembered his grief when he'd thought the document had been destroyed: and then his joy when he'd discovered it was safe. He remembered Miss Fanny's hopes in it—not much less than his own. And now? Not even a "whereas" or a "felonious" or a "property" to justify a family's dreams. Good God, and the old man had been killed for it!

"The discovery . . . the discovery," whispered Mr. Mansfield. "What was it?"

"Took it with 'im to the grave," said Smith, dully. "Dead man's wish. To be respected. Remember?"

Mr. Mansfield shook his head. "We must know it, Smith. There'll be no peace otherwise."

"You find out on your own, Mister Mansfield. I'm done with it. I'm off."

"But I'm blind, Smith. I—I need your eyes."

"Your daughter's eyes are just as sharp."

"Not so. They're partial. They're dimmed by affection. Yours, Smith, are vastly clear."

Smith, whose eyes were, at that time, anything but clear, being misted with tears of disappointment and general dissatisfaction with the world, nodded.

"True enough."

Mr. Mansfield frowned, and his projecting brows hid his empty eyes in pools of darkness so that, to an ignorant glance, he was no more blind than the boy.

"What did you hope for from the document? Great riches? Power? What was it, Smith, that you struggled for so hugely?"

Smith did not answer: partly on account of an obscure anger against the magistrate, and partly because he'd never had a clear notion of what he'd hoped for . . . save to make his way up in the world.

Mr. Mansfield waited, seeming to stare into the fire. Little by little, his head sank once more onto his chest. Smith watched him. Surely, he was asleep? Maybe half an hour passed . . .

"Smith!"

"I'm 'ere."

"I thought you'd gone. You said you were going. Have you changed your mind?"

"I'll go in the morning."

Once more there was silence: a long silence, broke only by the crackling of the fire and the blind man's regular breathing. Desolate, Smith stared at the unlucky document. The words jiggled and danced before his tired eyes

—but never again to shape themselves into the mystery of hope.

Why had the old man been killed? As if it mattered! He was dead as mutton! Smith frowned. In the morning he'd be off and the document, the dead man, and the blind man would be left behind. Tomorrow, the Town again—with its subtle alleys and sleepy pockets. Back to the beginning.

As if that was possible! Most miserably, Smith knew there could be no returning. Wherever he went, whatever he did, Curtis Court and its long consequences would haunt him. What had the old man discovered—and why had he been so coldly done in?

The blind man had been right. There'd be no peace for Smith till he knew. And little by little, as he sat—or rather, crouched—by the smallish fire, the desire to uncover the mystery of Mr. Field's dread became as strong as his first desire to read the document itself.

No more snow had fallen in the night, and now a bloodless, bewildered-looking sun stood poised on the Eastern hills—as if one nudge of a cloud would topple it into snowy oblivion. Everywhere, there was an air of universal crystallization for a frost had overlaid the snow, icing the ice and setting, on the fatted twigs of bushes, trees, and thickets, tiny needles that glinted sharply, blue, green, and orange . . .

Sometimes, these bushes took on the shapes of men, unhorsed and frozen as they'd stumbled on: here was a fellow with a slouched hat; there, one with a great nose and a pipe; and there was another, brandishing a huge pistol, fixed for the winter in a murderous aggression . . .

Somberly, Smith wondered if such a fate had befallen Lord Tom and the two men in brown: for he and Mr.

Mansfield were on the last stage of their singular journey to Prickler's Hill, and Smith was as watchful as a hawk.

He sat atop the coach beside the wounded coachman, who was now recovered enough—he swore—to hold the reins in his right hand: though he looked to Smith for help and support whenever the coach tipped. He'd been vastly surprised to see the "weasel" in his master's company—and had inadvertently said so, much confusing Charlie Parkin.

" 'Weasel'? But I understood his name was 'Jones.' I've writ down 'Jones.' "

"Jones? He's 'Smith'!" declared the coachman.

"Jones!" said Mr. Mansfield.

"Smith-Jones-Weasel . . ." muttered Charlie. "There's more to this than meets the eye!"

"There is indeed!" agreed Mr. Mansfield: and to this day, the constable never knew why the blind man laughed.

But now they were nearing the end of their journey. They skirted the village of Whetstone—and still no sign of pursuers.

"The House!" said the coachman, jerking his head toward the eminence of Prickler's Hill.

The House, built in the Palladian style, stood a third of the way up the hill, sheltered from the north by rising ground, and separated from Whetstone by an old stone church whose tombyard, shrouded in snow, was the very image of white and peaceful sleep.

The coach could go no further. The road was steep and vilely slippery. The horses steamed and labored in vain.

"On foot, then," said Mr. Mansfield: and he bade the coachman return into Whetstone while he and Smith went forward on foot.

"Pistols, Mister Mansfield? Shall I take 'em?"

The magistrate shook his head. "The gentlemen from Highgate Hill seem to've given up. No need for weapons now."

Smith shrugged his shoulders, took Mr. Mansfield's hand, and began the last ascent: and, though he could see nothing uneasy anywhere in the white landscape, he could not rid himself of the feeling that they were being watched closely. Where from? The House? The village? Or from the quiet churchyard? He said nothing of this to Mr. Mansfield, there being no sense in alarming the blind man without just cause. Instead, he listened and commented as Mr. Mansfield talked of Mr. Field and his unlucky life: but all the while, never gave up his searching, uneasy looks . . .

Thus, he learned with but half a mind about the disappearance and most likely death of Mr. Field's only son some years before, which had been followed by so relentless a siege of the old man and his property by his brothers, their wives and children that . . .

". . . that what, Mister Mansfield?"

"That there were suspicions—grim suspicions—that the eager family knew more than they said about the son's death."

Smith sighed. "D'you think that could have been the old man's discovery, Mister Mansfield? That he found out for certain what they'd done?"

Mr. Mansfield had been about to answer, when he frowned at a sudden, strong pressure from Smith's hand.

"What is it, Smith?"

"Nothing. Just the cold."

Smith stared deeply toward the churchyard. He was tolerably certain he'd seen something shift, slightly and secretly . . .

T HOUGH MR. FIELD was now many weeks dead, there was still a bereaved—even fatherless—air about his house. Dogs barked as the blind man and the boy trudged along the short curved drive, but no one bade them be quiet—or came to see why they barked. Five yards from the door, Smith faltered.

"What is it? The cold again?"

"Freezing!" said Smith. He had fancied that he'd seen a movement in the tombyard, now below.

The barking of the unseen dogs grew louder, and to Smith it seemed they were warning, not the house, but the blind man and him to keep away . . . to avoid . . . not to come closer . . . to abandon whatever it was that had brought them across the snow. "Go back! Back! Monstrousness is here! Wickedness is here! The Devil is here!"

But it was too late! They'd been seen approaching. The tall door opened and a footman received them. At the sound of the door the dogs fell silent, and the footman nodded.

"The master's beasts, sir. There's no hushing them till they hear the door. The ignorant creatures still believe he will come back, and only when they hear the door do they understand he's not come yet. For he always went to them first. Poor, ignorant beasts, God help them!"

Yet Smith felt that the footman was oddly proud of the "ignorant beasts," and maybe thought them not so ignorant after all. He was old, but still upright, though the worn shine of his livery across his back betrayed a straining—even a longing—to bow at last. He took Mr. Mansfield's card, lowering his eyes to read it as if to avoid the blind man's stare.

"Yes—yes, of course, sir! I should have known you! You have been before."

"Long ago."

"Long ago, sir."

Now they were in the hall of Mr. Field's house—and Smith stared about him as if the discovery that unlucky old man had made was written somewhere on the walls . . . or was being whispered from the faintly jingling chandelier. But the walls betrayed nothing: only some ghostly pale patches where pictures had once hung . . .

"Grand paintings used to be there!" said the servant, with ancient pride, seeing Smith's looks.

"I remember them well," said Mr. Mansfield, softly. "I remember a King Saul and David . . ."

"Aye, sir. That was the first to go."

"To go?"

"Sold, sold, sold, sir . . . to pay the butcher, the baker and . . ."

". . . and the chimney sweep down the road?" put in Smith, quickly.

The servant looked at him curiously: then shrugged his shoulders. "If you will, lad. The chimney sweep down the road—whoever he may be!"

"A gent with a wooden leg."

At this, the old servant seemed to stiffen and lose what little color the years had left him with. Then he recovered. An angry look came into his eyes and Smith knew he'd made an enemy of the old man. But for the life of him, he couldn't imagine why.

Mr. Mansfield enquired for Mr. Lennard: but it seemed the attorney was in Barnet and would not be at the house till midday. Indeed, there was no one in the house but Miss Field (the dead master's sister) and two of the nephews.

He said "No one" with a strong inflection, so that Miss Field and the nephews coming after did indeed seem part and parcel of "no one." Not that the old man had been contemptuous, but there was in his voice a weariness of something too well-known for contempt.

"The others are with Mister Lennard, sir. They are always with Mister Lennard. They give him no peace, sir—not even to conduct the business. He stayed here, sir, for two nights. But had to leave. They were at him all the while. They're sure he knows something he'll not tell them. Poor souls! They're in need even of the necessary penny to bless themselves with . . . and so will go to Hell! For who will bless them now? Not I! Not I!"

They were now come into the chief drawingroom: a

long, handsome room with tall windows giving out onto
the church and Whetstone beyond it. There was a fire in
the grate, but it burned cheerlessly, with uneasy flames
and little heat. Here, too, there were ghosts on the walls—
and a small writing table by one of the windows. At such a
table Mr. Field must have sat to write the document:
maybe this very one . . .

Was it here he'd wrote of the discovery that had sent
him hurrying to the Town? Or had the desperate family
sold that table, together with the pictures to—to pay the
chimney sweep down the road?

Smith stared somberly out of the window toward the
churchyard. Once more, he had the feeling of being secretly watched.

"Not I!" said the servant for a third time, and his grim
sentiment was not to be answered.

"You are a hard fellow," said Mr. Mansfield, sternly:
for hardness begets hardness.

"I am an old man, sir: and in the course of Nature, I'll
soon be with my master. *Then* I'll make my reckoning
with the Almighty: but before that, I must finish my account with Mister Field. Though he is dead, sir, my duty
to him is not."

He assisted Mr. Mansfield to a chair which the blind
man being unused to the hands that were guiding him, felt
carefully and exactly. He frowned. The upholstery was
much torn: a strange state of affairs in so short a time since
the master's death.

But it was not that chair alone: everywhere in the room
cushions and seats were in a grievous state, their white
insides peeping forth for all the world as though the wild,
pervasive snow had crept into the house and hid itself
everywhere.

"Aye," said the servant. " 'Tis the same elsewhere. You'll not find a cushion, chair covering nor bolster un-slit: nor a floorboard unopened: nor a wall unransacked for a secret opening. The family have been hard at it, for they've a heathenish belief the master hid a great fortune somewhere against the chance of—of poor dead Jack's returning! But Jack will come back when his father does —and that will be at the Judgment of us all! Not a day before! Aye! and *then* the beasts will bark and bark!"

("But where did Jack play as a boy?" Smith suddenly wondered—with an excitement he'd almost forgot.)

Now the servant—after brushing some ash from the hearth, on which the fire looked more wretched than ever —left the room to announce Mr. Mansfield to Miss Field. Smith and the blind man were alone.

"Andrews!" muttered Smith, urgently. "We'd best ask Andrews where Jack played as a boy!"

"Why? D'you still have your hopes? If so, forget them, Smith. We'll wait for Mister Lennard."

The blind man spoke sharpishly, as if Smith had sud-denly lost ground with him. He breathed deeply—and provoked a silence. Then he said abruptly:

"Where are you now?"

"By the fire."

"Oh yes—yes . . ."

"Why did you ask?"

"I—I thought you were over there." He pointed to the windows. "I thought you were staring at me."

But before Smith could answer, Miss Field came hur-riedly into the room. She was a gaunt-boned, elderly lady—large, though frail and anxious-looking. She rustled tremendously as she moved: like great sweepings of au-tumn leaves.

"Mister Mansfield! Kate Field at your service, sir!"

She held out a hand, looked puzzled when it wasn't took—then flushed at her mistake and glanced apologetically at Smith, as if she'd wounded *him*.

"Sad times, Mister Mansfield! A brother dead . . . the family penniless! Sell, sell, sell! But we must! To live, you know! I expect you've noticed great changes—oh!" Once more she flushed, and bit her lip. "But how's dear little Rose? It—it *is* Rose, isn't it, sir?"

She seemed particularly anxious to get *something* right and was much relieved when the blind man nodded. So she went breathlessly on, shifting about the room—even picking at the ruined funrnishings—like a large black moth in search of a meal.

She faintly resembled her murdered brother, and this touched Smith curiously, so that when she returned—as she often did—to the family's distress and disappointed hopes and desperation for money, he could not share the blind man's indifference. Why shouldn't the silly old woman long for money? And be open about it? Steeped as he was in the darknesses of the Town, Smith understood too well Miss Field's painful distraction—that had pushed out even seemly grief at her brother's death.

Abruptly, Miss Field realized she was not recommending herself to anyone but the curious urchin the magistrate had brought with him: so she cast a rapid, melancholy smile at Smith and began to talk hurriedly and sadly about the dead man.

"Yes—yes . . . a sad life, my brother's! A tragedy, Mister Mansfield! Never, never for a day did he get over the loss of Jack! Never accepted it. The shock, I suppose. Always expected him to come riding up the drive! Tragic! Even turned on the rest of us when we tried to tell him!

Tragic for *us*! *We* only meant to help! And—and believe me, it was for the best!" (Here, she glanced uneasily at the servant as if she suspected him of something worse than contempt.) "Not a worthy son! Not likeable. Though I was his Aunt, I say it . . . and God forgive me. Better off dead! But—but we mustn't speak ill of them . . . the dead, I mean, for there they lie—" (She was by the window, momentarily looking out.) "—in the churchyard. My brother—his dear wife—Well, well! Maybe he's with his precious Jack in Heaven now!" (She glanced almost defiantly at the servant, who turned away.) "And maybe he repents of having hid his fortune away from us! Cruel, cruel thing to do! Unnatural, don't you think, Mister Mansfield?"

Mr. Mansfield lips were tight—and Smith was sorry for it. He was, at that time, sorry for a great many things: not least that the long search and deep pursuit should end in his cheerless, ransacked house with the pitiful old lady somehow driving a deeper wedge than ever between him and the implacable blind man . . .

"*Our* tragedy, Mister Mansfield! It's all *our* tragedy! Everyone turns against us! Even Attorney Lennard. Oh, I can tell! He turns away—he frowns—he would not stay here. *God knows* what he thinks of us all! You come at a sad time, sir! And all on account of the money! And where *is* it? *God knows* we've done our part! *God knows* we've searched!" (She stared at the torn furnishings.) "Oh it's cruel! And yet it *must* be somewhere—ah!"

She stopped as a far-off tumbling was heard. "Nephews in the attic, sir! Must go! Pray to God they've found something! Pray to *God*!"

She was already half through the door when she remembered her responsibilities. "Do forgive me, sir! Mind on other things! Our tragedy, you know! Serve wine, Andrews!"

With that she was gone, leaving Smith to stare, dismayed, at the old servant of whom he'd made an enemy: at Andrews, who held the key to one secret, at least.

"Ask him!" breathed Smith—desperately—into the blind man's ear as Andrews was at a side table. But the magistrate grimly shook his head.

Back came Andrews with a glass of wine for Mr. Mansfield—and for Smith a deeply hostile look. So Smith returned to staring restlessly and unhappily through the windows. An obscure feeling of haste was gripping him . . . as if he'd been infected by the general unquiet of the house itself. Outside, the churchyard was hid by snow-hatted yews. But up stood the bell tower on tiptoe—with an air of stony peering . . .

Andrews was talking with Mr. Mansfield . . . about Jack. Defending the dead son against the unjust attack. Andrews was very jealous of the dead's good name: both father and son. For the living, he'd not so much to say. And the blind man was nodding gravely as he heard how well and handsomely Jack had grown to manhood—instead of asking Andrews where Jack had played as a boy! "Dead man's wishes!" Smith longed to cry out. "To be respected! Ask of Andrews where Jack used to play as a boy!"

"It's twelve years, now," Andrews went on. "And still they've not forgiven him for being beloved! Still they dislike him, abuse him, hate and envy him—as if he will indeed come riding up the drive and snatch some trifle out of their greedy hands!"

"Is it twelve years already, Andrews?"

Twelve years it was, and Jack had been just twenty,

with the world before him. And then—he'd vanished. Gone into London, it was supposed, and been swallowed up. There was a tale he'd been pressed aboard a ship that had gone down with all hands. But did it matter now? After twelve years, the dead lie deep—and it's only their good name that can be distressed.

"So why can't they let him rest in peace with his father?" Andrews nodded to the windows and beyond: and the peering belfry seemed to nod back. Yet the yews had a secret air . . . These yews were not so close together as Smith had at first supposed. Here and there, there were thin gaps . . . Was it from these gaps that came the sense of watching?

"I'll leave you now, sir," Andrews was saying, and Smith's desperation grew extreme. He sensed that Mr. Mansfield was lost to him. All that remained was "the trifle." Such hopes as he had, had dwindled to that, and he clung to them as if for his life. It was eleven o'clock. The attorney was to come at midday. Smith believed he'd an hour remaining. (But the time was shorter than he dreamed.)

"Mister Andrews!" he cried out.

The servant's hand was on the door. He paused.

"Tell us—what was Jack like as—as a boy?"

"Smith!" muttered the magistrate, warningly.

But Andrews, for some reason, turned to answer.

"Why, he was well-built: very well-built. Handsome. Oh yes! And thoughtful. He was of a thoughtful disposition."

"Were 'e like me, then?"

"He was—country bred." (With a sneer)

"D'you mean 'e didn't run an' climb and play like—like other lads?" went on Smith—who'd done none of these things, save run. "Didn't 'e 'ave no favorite places to nip into when the going was hot? Didn't 'e 'ave no little alley or court 'e could call 'is own, Mister Andrews?"

"Smith!" whispered the blind man, fiercely.

"For if 'e didn't, Mister Andrews, 'e weren't a very natural boy!"

Andrews—touched on a raw place—answered almost contemptuously:

"Where you, boy, might make a nest in a dirty corner of the wicked Town, Jack, when the secret mood was on him (such as comes to all boys who love to dream), would go—"

"—where? Where would 'e go?" (Smith's excitement was intense. So near—so near!)

"Smith—"

But Andrews had already crossed the room. Not even the furious magistrate could prevent him defending the dead Jack's quality against the urchin. With wide eyes, Smith watched him. He halted by the window. He pointed —and Smith's blood chilled!

"There was Jack's nest! In yonder churchyard—by the statue of a carved black angel. *There* he'd sit and dream his dreams—and, maybe, even watch us all . . ."

Andrews was gone from the room. Mr. Mansfield had heard him take his leave.

"Smith!" he whispered, urgently. No answer. "Smith! Smith! Where are you?"

Silence and darkness . . . deeper than the blind man had ever known it. The boy was gone!

He rose to his feet and began, with desperate haste, to feel his way toward the last sound he'd heard: the door. The empty air mocked at him—offering the feeling of obstacles, then declaring "nothing here, blind man!" as he jerked and staggered, then thankfully struck against the wall.

"Smith! Smith! Come back! You're mad, child! You'll damn yourself! No one will help you now! Smith!"

He found the door, opened it—and felt cold air blowing in his face. This, he knew he must follow. He prayed to God no one would see him as he tottered foolishly, ridiculously after the thieving, too-clever urchin to whom he seemed uncannily chained.

"Smith . . . Smith!" he kept whispering into what he imagined were corners: in the hope the child was hiding from him—was playing a cruel game—was only pretending to be gone to the damnable churchyard to dig up "the trifle"—to be gone forever into the implacable silence and dark. "Voices in the night," he'd said on a certain terrible day. Did he know the truth of it? And did he know what the dark was like when the voices were gone? Did he know the *other* voices that plague a blind man?

"Smith . . . Smith . . ."

He was now very near the source of the cold air. He heard a chandelier jingling as a draft stirred it. He was in the hall. The front door was open.

"Smith!" he called helplessly: and fell out into the snow. Much shaken, he struggled upright.

"Smith!" he cried out, as loudly as he dared: for he was committed too deeply with the invisible, infant criminal to court any other's knowledge of it. He'd perjured himself for him: he'd given up a dead man's trust to him: he'd broken the law and compromised his own honor for him: he'd wrecked himself for him—and because of what? Wretchedly, he shook his head—and the snow fell away from his hair. "Child! Come back to me! Smith—I'm frightened . . . for you . . . for me! Smith . . ."

No answer—nothing but the restless motion of cold air through unseen shrubs . . . Then a dog began to bark— then another, and another! A shrill, dreadful sound in the blind man's ears: for the creatures now sounded ferocious, as if warning of a new crisis in the house's affairs which they, if they were loosed, could avert. Was it him they would tear and snap at? Or was there someone else on his way?

Suddenly, a hand clutched at his wrist and dragged him furiously to one side! Smith had come back!

"Smith—"

"Quiet! Someone's on 'is way! The ignorant beasts 'ave gone mad again!" Smith's voice was low and trembling. He sounded frightened half to death! Had he already been to the churchyard?

"Child—"

"Quiet, I tell you!" His grip on the blind man's wrist was almost vicious in its strength—as if the boy was exacting such small vengeance as he could for having been drawn back. For Smith conceived with dread that the dogs were barking the approach of the two men in brown!

He'd seen the blind man swaying in the drive. He'd heard him calling. But had not moved till the dogs barked. So where had he been, so still and quiet and unbreathing, even? By the gate of the churchyard . . . staring into the snow. Certain footprints had appalled him: frozen him body and soul. Till he'd seen the helpless Mr. Mansfield— and heard the warning dogs.

"Where are you dragging me, child?"

"To the churchyard."

"Why?"

"You'll see."

"Have you forgotten—I'm blind?"

"Not that blind, Mister Mansfield."

The dogs were still barking. Whoever was coming was not yet near enough to disappoint them. Smith fancied he heard a carriage door . . . but still he dragged Mr. Mansfield through the concealing bushes, enjoining him to the absolutest quiet. For there was yet more to fear than whatever the dogs barked at: and yet more to discover than ever those creatures would learn.

Down, down to the churchyard—with the snow flurrying secretly about them—hurried the boy and the blind man, till they were at the gate. The blind man felt the boy halt a moment: he felt his fingers tremble and grip tighter than ever before: heard him draw in his breath. Then they went inside . . .

Vastly still and silent was the little garden where the dead were planted and bloomed in stone. Very prettily did the headstones wear their widows' caps of snow, and stand respectfully in groups and rows . . .

But even in death there's ambition, and a carved black angel knelt upon one tomb as if to say, "What a special one lies here!" Now this angel knelt upon a flat stone to which mounted three steps. Upon these steps was a second figure: still enough to be likewise carved. A figure with an easy, familiar air—as if he was come back at last to a place much loved in childhood. The figure of a man with a wooden leg . . .

chapter NINETEEN

STILL KNOWING NOTHING for certain but the need for extreme secrecy, the blind man suffered himself to be pulled and dragged down till he felt the stone of the church at his back, and heard Smith's voice breathe close in his ear:

" 'e's there, by the statue! Peg top! Stilty! Old 'op-an'-Scape! Whispering Jack! Jack o' the alley! Little Jackie Field—and the spitting image of 'is done-for pa! It's my *Mister Green!*"

"The son! Alive?"

"Yes. More's the pity! It was 'im what done the old man in! Little limping whispering Jack!"

"Horrible, horrible!"

" 'e's not of yore opinion! For 'e's a-smiling, there! 'e's of a thoughtful disposition, 'e is! Country-bred. Who'd 'ave thought the Devil was born among the green fields out Barnet way? Yes—'e's a-smiling very thoughtful. You got no eyes, friend: and you should be thankful for you ain't missing much!"

So now they knew—beyond all doubt—what discovery the old man had made, and sought to take with him to the grave. He had discovered his son was still alive—and would have been better dead! That the hope, the dream, the golden place in his life was as wicked and monstrous a morsel of man and wood as stalked and whispered and hid anywhere in the world!

To this dreadful thing the document had at last led Smith and Mr. Mansfield: to this one-legged gentleman, squatting in the shadow of a carved angel's wing, smiling broodily, with the air of having come by appointment . . . Fearfully, Smith's mind went back to his one-time hopes that the document would raise him up in the world. Instead, it had given him a sight of depths past even his darkest dreams.

But the one-legged gentleman was looking up. Someone was coming . . . keeping the appointment. Who'd arranged to meet with the Devil?

" 'ere 'e comes!" breathed Smith, with bitter triumph. "Yore friend and mine."

Into the churchyard, skipping across the snow with his black coattails flapping—like a prosperous bird of prey— came the neat Mr. Billing!

"Jack!" he called gently.

"Billing!" (Mr. Mansfield stiffened, as if to rise. Grimly, Smith held him back. He would have the magistrate hear all there was to be heard.)

"The document. Have you got it?" (This, from Mr. Billing who was come to "Mr. Green's" side.)

"No. Our brown friends are not yet come."

"Ah well, it won't be long now, dear Jack!"

Mr. Billing laid his hand round the other's shoulder. The one-legged man seemed to shiver slightly—as if submitting with an ill grace . . . being lame.

"As you say, not long, dear Billing . . . and we'll be rid of each other!"

"Why Jack! We're friends! Have been so for years! Why the bitterness—now?"

"You made me kill him, Billing!"

"*I* made you? Jack, Jack, it's not so!"

"*You* planned! *You* urged! *You* tempted!"

"Ah! but *you* acted, Jack! Never forget that!"

"How can I? Not till I die! And maybe not even then!" (He looked up at the black angel—then back to the attorney with a harsh groan.) "And d'you remember, you even swore it would be Andrews coming."

"A murder's a murder, Jack—no matter who perishes. But don't blame yourself, dear! It's not you—or me. It's this world we live in, Jack! What can we do? We've got to live. Take the rough with the smooth, Jack. It'll all come out in the wash! If there's a God in Heaven, He knows the difficulties we're up against down here. He'll understand. He'll forgive us! And—if there's no such Judge—well, Jack, what have we got to lose? It's all in the mind, my dear! Well, well—we'd all like to be saints through and through! Nothing nicer! But we can't. It's the world, Jack, not us! And we can't change that! No, sir!"

In the quiet, cold air the voices carried intimately, so's no inflection, even, was lost on the listeners. Not Mr. Green, but Mr. Billing was the Devil! Mr. Green was but the outward image of evil—its eyes, teeth, hands, skin, and hair: but Mr. Billing was its inward, horrible, cajoling, obliging soul!

They continued murmuring in a like vein for a while longer: and it became plain it was not for the first time. There was a weariness in Mr. Green's bitterness, and a boredom in the attorney's evasions that bespoke much repetition. And over and above them the black angel brooded thoughtfully . . . and somewhere beneath them lay whatever it was they'd murdered for. The buried trifle.

But now a slight breeze sprang up, lifting little tufts of snow from the stones, as if there was a restlessness below . . . a stirring . . .

"Oh God for judgment!" groaned Mr. Mansfield. "But what sort of Judgment can there be?"

"At last!" exclaimed Mr. Green. "They're come!"

And Mr. Billing smiled and waved.

From the far end of the churchyard, through the quiet yews, came the two men in brown! Very dark-faced and frozen were they, as they approached their employers. But the breeze quickened, and their exchanges were partly lost.

". . . the document?"

". . . not got it!"

". . . not? Why not? Not killed the blind man, then? Not managed even . . . trifle?"

They shook their wicked heads. Mr. Green—gray with terror and rage—raised his hand to strike at them! But Mr. Billing—everyone's friend—stayed his hand. And did not free it. Grasped at his wrist: forced it down . . . and made it point! (Would Mr. Billing have used even his own finger? Not if another was at hand!) Pointed to the snow.

What was so remarkable about the snow? Footmarks. There were his own. There—so curious that they'd chilled Smith's blood when he'd first spied them—were the one-legged man's. And—and oh yes—another pair of pairs not accounted for. Leading through the gate. (How the held hand shook as it was urged from the wrist to point and follow!)

Through the gate. Close by the church wall. To a certain old tree . . .

"They've found us!" whispered Smith. "We ain't got a chance, Mister Mansfield! Judgment's come all right—but it's come for us!"

Slowly, the two men in brown turned to peer at the tree. Then a single grin spread over their murderers' faces. They began to walk.

The breeze grew into a wind and the snow about their feet shuddered and shifted as if there was a creeping turmoil below.

"Kill them!" screamed Mr. Billing, abruptly. "No help for it! You've got to do it!"

Could Smith have escaped? In all certainty, yes! He'd the agility, the quickness, the wit, and the terror to vanish from the abominable churchyard before the men had covered half the distance. But not so Mr. Mansfield. The old mole-in-the-hole could never have got further than the gate without a sharp knife in his broad back. So Smith, with all his quickness, wit, and terror, lacked the last ingredient for flight: the will. He was not capable of leaving the blind man behind.

Maybe the God of Forgiveness will take this into account when the time comes . . . and with it cancel out all Smith's sins and imperfections?

"They're a-coming, Mister Mansfield!"

"Then for God's sake, go!"

"For God's sake? That's a queer thing!"

The men were now very close. They carried short, glittering knives. Already, they could see Smith—and were grinning widely—even encouragingly—at him.

Smith, in spite of all his knowledge of the worst of the Town—its rogues and vagrants, its thieves and slinking byways—was really no more than a child . . . and he turned to childish weapons for his last defense. With small, trembling fingers he made a snowball, stood up, and with a loud, defiant shriek, flung it at the nearer of the advancing pair!

The man swore—but stopped! His companion (instead of dispatching the boy) first laughed. A very costly laugh, that. The seconds thus spent were important.

Momentarily, the wind puffed up a little storm of snow and out of it—as if resurrected from under the white ground itself—staggered a formidable figure!

"Stop! Hold! Stand, there!"

Cloaked, large, hugely pistoled: Lord Tom!

"You dirty great bag of wind! Be off with you!" snarled the man with snow in his face.

"Spare the boy! I'll—I'll not have him harmed!"

"*You'll* not? And who's *you,* Lord-piddling-Tom? Be off—or we'll slit you in tiny pieces, friend!"

Lord Tom's frostily bristling face grew pitifully angry.

"Smut!" he called, waving vaguely. "Never fear! Lord Tom's beside you! I'll save you, lad! I'll blow blue daylight through 'em!"

"Be off, Lord Tom!" answered Smith, bitterly. "You'd best save your own lousy skin. I'm done with you now! I know you, Lord Tom. And I don't like what I know!"

The huge highwayman flinched. He screwed up his little

eyes. Whether or not he really loved the boy was hard to say. Maybe he did. Maybe the sharp wound he'd just received was all but mortal. And so, maybe from this moment on, he was fighting for more than his life: he was fighting for his immortal soul . . . (What was Mr. Green fumbling in his coat for?)

"Back! Back!" shouted Lord Tom, with the utmost valor and rage.

"And if we don't?" sneered the two men.

"Then you're dead as mutton!"

For a second time, the smaller of the two men in brown laughed. He steadied his knife. Took a pace forward—

"Blue daylight!" roared Lord Tom—and fired!

A terrible, double roar: a terrible, double shout! The man who laughed—laughed no more. He was dead. And Lord Tom—Lord Tom, much astonished, was capering foolishly in the snow, opening and shutting his mouth in defiant shouts that emerged as silent puffs of scarlet air!

There was a ball inside of him: Mr. Green had shot him even as he'd discharged his own pistol. Lord Tom was as good as dead: but he seemed not to know it yet. Instead, with the meager remains of his life he threatened the second of the two men with a pistol that was suddenly grown marvelously heavy. And this second fellow, seeing his companion dead, waited no longer. Savagely, he rushed away.

Lord Tom's dance grew slower and most comically clumsy as he strove to lift his great boots out of the clinging snow. Even as the amazed (and suddenly heartbroken) Smith watched, all the fire and fury and daring rage drained out of his old hero's face. He halted, tottering . . . then sank upon his knees, curiously crossing his pistols upon his chest where there was a warm, gushing pain . . .

"Ha-ha! Blue daylight, eh, lad?"

They were alone in the graveyard now. Mr. Green had hopped crazily in the wake of his adviser and friend. They'd heard sounds from the house. The shots had set up an alarm. The dogs were yelping in a tragical frenzy—

Lord Tom lay with his head on the lowest of the steps where Mr. Green had sat and waited. Above him brooded the black angel. If he knew he was done for the sight must have frightened him. Yet he showed none of it. Sadly, Smith approached him, leading blind Mr. Mansfield.

"Glad to make your—acquaintance, sir! Never—never thought to! Ha-ha! Shake hands? Really, an honor—"

"And for me, Lord Tom. And for me!"

Solemnly, their hands, guided by Smith, met and grasped: the dying highwayman's and the blind magistrate's. And both were glad ot it . . . for both had reached the end of a journey: Lord Tom's was his last—but Mr. Mansfield's was, maybe, his first. A very strange journey: from justice to compassion.

Now Lord Tom closed his eyes, and from out of his side a red patch blossomed in the snow, spread . . . gently melted into tiny scarlet needles and caves . . . then filled up.

"Nights on the Common, Smut!" he whispered. "Duval . . . Turpin . . . Robinson . . . and—and—"

"—and Lord Tom!" wept Smith: for his friend was dead.

And so was "Mr. Green." Andrews had followed him. Seen him leaping and hopping away. Very easy to see in the snow. Shapes like Mr. Green's show up very plain and black. He'd taken a fowling piece and gone after him. Caught him this side of Whetstone. And shot him dead.

He lay like a malformed dark star in the snow—a giant child's star, with a wooden stick to hold it by . . . that shadowy, formidable ruin of a good man's son.

What had been his history? As dark and shadowy as the rest of him. Where had he lived, how lost his leg, how met with his corrupt adviser? Questions to which there were never answers. All that was known for certain was that he'd fled his home twelve years before and never dared return on account of some hanging offense. This, Andrews knew of, and preferred that the world and Mr. Field should think Jack dead rather than damned. A heavy secret—and the granity old fellow's shoulders were bending under it. But to hide an evil is not to destroy it. The old man had made his discovery . . . and had been hurried into his grave.

Andrews must have stood a great while upon a hillock above the fallen figure—for when Mr. Lennard's coach came toward Prickler's Hill, he was still there, looking to the sky as if the spread shape below had fallen a great way to this cold, white ruin.

But of Mr. Billing there was no sign, and it seemed for a while as though the earth itself had swallowed him up. No one saw him—neither anyone in the house, nor Mr. Lennard coming from Barnet, nor Miss Mansfield coming a-foot from Whetstone, where Mr. Billing (whom she'd insisted on accompanying) had begged her to remain: as if to spare her from the tragic news he was confident was awaiting—that her father had been murdered on Finchley Common. For there was no doubt that this vile and hateful man still loved Miss Mansfield: for the sake of which spark of humanity in him, maybe his sentence in the courts of Heaven will be to burn in Hell for one day less than if he'd never loved at all.

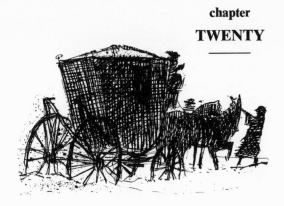

MOURNFUL SMITH, Smith of disasters, Smith who'd led the blind so fatefully . . . storm-tossed, heartbroken Smith! He stared through the windows of the house to the widowy yew trees behind which lay his idol, Lord Tom— fallen, then risen only to fall again.

His snow-stained, tear-stained face came but rarely out of its faraway looking to survey the busy drawingroom: and only the most serious commotion could hold him for long. The coming of Mr. Lennard, together with as many of the old man's family as could get into his coach, interested him but little: and even Mr. Mansfield's proud introduction of him to the old-fashioned lawyer with his old-fashioned face ("My guardian angel, sir! A little singed and tattered about the wings—but then he's flown through the caves of Hell! Meet Smith."), even this grand introduction provoked but a melancholy smile.

"Pleased to meet you, I am sure," he muttered. And turned back to the viewing of his private grief. "Lord Tom —Lord Tom! You blew blue daylight through 'em . . . just like you said! Oh Lord Tom—you went like the grandest toby of them all!")

Cowardice, boastfulness, and double-dealing had bled out of Lord Tom into the snow: and what remained in Smith's heart was "the grandest toby of them all."

Then Miss Mansfield came—and Smith turned and smiled compassionately across the room at her. For she'd learned of Mr. Billing's monstrousness, and the pain and bitterness in her heart was written in her eyes. Quickly, she crossed to the window, put her arm about Smith's shoulder and pressed her cold face to his, so that her dark hair curtained them off in a private night.

"Sorry you lost a friend, miss," he said. Then turned away even from her, to the dark yew trees and the strangely moving whiteness beyond.

"Smith," murmured Mr. Mansfield, who had not left his side. "What did he—look like?"

Smith sniffed and swallowed hard. " 'e was a big man, Mister Mansfield . . . and always wore green. Green 'at, green cloak, green breeches—and 'e'd bright green eyes as well! 'e bristled a bit about the chops—but 'ad such a smile on 'im when he talked of the Common that 'e fair shone! 'e was a real gallant 'igh toby, Mister Mansfield. One of the best!"

"He—went well, Smith."

"None better, Mister Mansfield."

"He's in Heaven, Smith."

"If there's Commons up there, that's where 'e is, Mister Mansfield. Right up 'igh on the snaffling lay!"

Then Mr. Lennard came over, followed by the inquisitive eyes of Mr. Field's family—the beneficiaries of nothing in particular. He began to talk in low tones to Mr. Mansfield, and Smith's mournful attention drifted away. Till a piece of sardonic humor struck him . . . a wry, Smith-like humor.

Mr. Mansfield was mentioning his name, and handing over the document to Mr. Lennard. With an awful smile Smith watched the stained and tattered paper change hands. In a moment it was done.

"Bleeding mailboy, that's what I been!" he brooded. "Documents took and delivered. No charge. And you may 'ave confidence. I'll rent me an office in the shadow of St. Paul's. Come wind, come snow, come Newgate Jail and the deaths of friends—Smith gets through with the documents! From Curtis Court to Prickler's Hill in less than three months! Well done, Smith!"

But Mr. Lennard had come now to "the trifle." Mild interest tickled Smith in spite of his aching heart. It was proposed to go at once to the burying place. Smith sighed. He'd no wish to visit that spot so soon. But the beneficiaries were eager . . .

"Come, Smith," murmured Mr. Mansfield, hearing sounds of movement to the door. "Let's see it out."

So Smith, still heavy of heart, but nonetheless inquisitive enough not to be left behind, followed the respectfully hopeful beneficiaries to the sheeted churchyard. Strange occasion, strange procession: to go to a churchyard in hope.

Through the well-remembered little gate they wound, past the rents in the snow where the dead man in brown and the mortality of Lord Tom had been decently dragged away.

" 'e's gone," whispered Smith: and Mr. Mansfield took off his hat.

Black and peaceful was the angel—undisturbed at its mysterious devotions though the world had rocked and tumbled about it.

"Is this the place?"

Andrews nodded. This was the place.

The sexton was fetched from the church—and, under a host of desperate eyes, began to dig . . .

Strangely like the old man himself were the crowding beneficiaries, thought Smith, as he watched them moving their lips in silent prayer. Like echoes of him: there was his nose, there his chin—and there, in his frail, gaunt sister, were his very eyes . , . Indeed, it was as though Mr. Field was come back to see his wishes at last fulfilled.

And now Smith turned to watch the toiling sexton who'd pierced the snow and was a foot into the frozen earth. He paused to wipe his brow. Hard on the beneficiaries—to wait while he drew breath. He grunted, and continued.

"Ah! What 'ave we 'ere?"

A straining forward: a vast excitement.

"No. Nothing. A slab of stone. Sorry, good people."

A general perishing of excitement. A gloom, almost. Old Miss Field had begun to weep. Smith bowed his small, storm-tossed head. Was everyone to be disappointed?

"Ah! What 'ave we 'ere?"

The sexton was looking up—frowning. What had been buried and not by him? A trifle. A wooden box . . . a traveling box . . .

"It was *his!*" whispered Miss Field. "I know it! He always used to take it with him to—"

"—but 'e's left it behind now, ma'am!" grunted the sexton, and struck off the strap with his spade.

It may be that it's unseemly for beneficiaries to beam and twinkle in a churchyard—to even caper gently in the snow and crowd and shake a lawyer's hand! But in God's name, what else were they to do? Crocodiles might have wept, but the beneficiaries were needy human souls.

Mr. Field's wooden box was filled, stuffed, and glutted with a prosperous lifetime's guineas! Guineas that lay upon guineas in sunny shoals, gleaming and winking in the cold light. The old man must have carried them there in bags which had long since split and sunk under the spreading weight of coinage: for, here and there, rufts of canvas poked up, like threads of cloud in a golden sky.

"A hundred thousand!" thought Smith, dreamily. "Must be a hundred thousand golden flatties down there! God save the King!" For Smith, whenever he saw a sight too grand for any of his words, always said, "God save the King!" (And sometime later that morning, when the company—in radiant spirits—were back in the house, he had occasion to say once more, "God save the King!")

It is night in the "Red Lion Tavern" between Turnmill Street and Saffron Hill. In the cellar Miss Fanny and Miss Bridget—reduced to four or five smoking tallows—are sewing mournfully. Miss Fanny has heard of the death of her admirer and is red-eyed and sniffy. Miss Bridget does not speak—but sighs and shrugs her shoulders from time to time. Their shadows hugely comment on them upon the wall. Miss Bridget looks up as if she will speak . . . but thinks better of it and returns to her work. Miss Fanny loudly sniffs again.

Suddenly, there are certain sounds from above. Miss Bridget frowns and shakes her head. (Her great shadow does likewise, as if in agreement.) But Miss Fanny puts down her work with an air of presentiment.

"It's 'im!"

"Never!"

"It's 'im, Brid! It's 'im!"

The door opens. There's a clatter and scuffle. Once more, Smith has missed his footing and fallen down the stairs!

"It's 'im! It's Smut!" cries Miss Fanny, dropping her work entirely and bustling to her feet.

"And about time, too!" says Miss Bridget, looking as stern as she might. "Oh you felonious child! We thought you was shamefully dead!"

Now Smith picks himself up, rubs his elbows, the side of his head and a shin. He squints disparagingly round the cellar, then grandly at his sisters.

"Dead?" he says. "What business would I 'ave being dead with ten thousands guineas to me name? Answer me that!"

And he stares at them with such an air of offended dignity and unnatural honesty, that they're half inclined to believe him. The half-so-inclined is Miss Fanny. The half which is not, is Miss Bridget—who's worked hard all of her young life and never dreamed of being related to more than twenty pound in cash.

Resolutely, she's ever set her handsome, but toil-stern self against her softer sister's imaginings, saying over and over again that such gaudy thoughts are as tinsel thread—

fit enough to decorate a bodice, but never to hold up a hem. Tears start to her thread-worn eyes as she sees her sister dote and smile foolishly upon the small Smith whose heart she thought she knew as being closer to her own.

Of a sudden, Miss Bridget feels tired and lonely in the seedy world of the "Red Lion's" cellar. "Why must it always be me," she thinks, "who's got to spoil the dreaming? Do they suppose I like this shameful place? But someone must face it out—for we can't live off dreams alone!"

"What would you say," says Smith, adding insult to injury by disengaging himself from Miss Fanny and coming to outface the stern Miss Bridget herself, "to a carriage an' pair, and a 'ouse in Golden Square?"

Miss Bridget looks at her silly sister and the thin child whose sharp face is fairly shining with pleasure. She sighs. "Why not?" she thinks. "What harm in a few hours of cheerful dreaming? Soon enough the gray, gray dawn." So Miss Bridget nods and smiles, and reaches out to ruffle Smith's head.

"I'd say, I'd like it very much. When do we move?"

"Tomorrow," says Smith. "And what would you say to a footman, a maid, and a coachie?"

"I'd say, very elegant, child. When do we engage them?" Is it possible Miss Bridget is beginning to enjoy the dreaming—or are her eyes shining only because she's warmed by Smith's generosity even in his dreams?

"Tomorrow," says Smith.

"Oh Smut!" cries Miss Fanny. "You are good! Might we have a tall coachman, in green livery?"

Smith nods in an offhand fashion. "And what would you say to offering me old friend Mister Magistrate Mansfield of Vine Street a tot of what might warm him against the cold night air?"

Miss Bridget smiles. "I'd say it would be an honor and we'd be very pleased to oblige. When do we invite 'im?"

"Now!" says Smith—and shouts: "Come in, Mister Mansfield! I prepared 'em! Mind the steps. There's thirteen!"

Upon which, Miss Fanny shrieks and Miss Bridget goes white as her stockings! For the door has opened and the great blind magistrate himself stands incredibly at the head of the stairs!

"Good evening, ladies. I've heard much about you."

Very pitiable to behold is now Miss Bridget for she's gone quite distracted and begins to fly about the cellar in a terrible frenzy of tidying and making seemly. Her thoughts are in a whirl and she knows not if she's on her head or her heels. She keeps crying out very breathlessly:

"Oh Smut! You should 'ave said—you should 'ave warned—oh Smut!"

Till Smith puts an end to her cellar-proud misery by saying:

"Don't fret, Miss Bridget. 'e's as blind as a mole. If it wasn't for the whiff, 'e might as well be in St. James's Palace! Ain't that so, Mister Mansfield?"

And the great man smiles and nods, and Miss Bridget is no longer in any doubt of which way up she is: she *knows* she is on her head!

And that was how Smith came home! Smith of the courts and alleys: Smith of the corners and byways and many a passing pocket! Smith the ten thousand guinea man! For he'd spoke not a half penny less than the truth!

On the morning at Prickler's Hill—to the beneficiaries' approval and his own speechless (save for 'God save the King!') delight—Attorney Lennard had awarded him one tenth of the churchyard treasure as a mark of gratitude and esteem: *Ten thousand* guineas!

"A good, round sum," had said Mr. Mansfield, with satisfaction. "And what are you going to do with it, Smith?" But Smith had answered never a word: he'd fainted away on "King!"

Small wonder, then, that Miss Bridget was distracted and, even after an hour with the magistrate sitting beside her talking gently and wisely of all their futures, still believed she'd fallen a victim to her sister's foolish dreaming and was no more awake than a bedpost!

But at last, when morning brought no gloomy fact to dispel the night's fancy, she permitted herself to believe that the future was a rosy and splendid affair . . . and even to tolerate, with a gracious smile, her sister's favorite remark, "I always said, Brid, that there was *some* good in our dockiment, didn't I?"

Though there was no more snow, the weather continued very cold until the beginning of March, when an unlooked-for warmth set in, and the sun came out in springlike glory. Everywhere, the snow—which had grown as flat, tired, and grubby as an old sheet—went into little green holes. Then, swiftly, these holes spread into islands which put out fingers, like children in a round dance, eager to touch their neighbors. So the green islands joined up and the whiteness shrank away till it vanished entirely, and nothing more was left of the snow but a crusty puddle or two in the vicinity of Godliman Street and Curtis Court, where Mr. Lennard, the attorney, has his office and sometimes works late . . . for he's short of a partner. Even though, one night, Mr. Billing came quietly and furtively back!

Much shocked, amazed and a trifle uneasy, Mr. Lennard let him in after warning him that he must and would have him arrested for his monstrous villainy.

"Don't be too harsh on me, sir!" Mr. Billing had muttered. With an apologetic smile. "It's this world we live in that's to blame! But believe me sir, I've come to make amends!"

Mr. Lennard stared at him—and Mr. Billing promptly declared his intention of turning King's Evidence! He knew where was the second murderer in brown: and, for the usual consideration, was prepared to give him up. The "usual consideration" was the sparing of his wretched life. Which, indeed, came to pass: for, though Mr. Billing's heart was black as pitch, his plump lawyer's hands were still as clean as snow . . .

There was nothing the justice of the law could do with him but sentence him to three years in Newgate Jail. Of which he served a month—and then fell an odd victim . . .

The old man who dwelt in the fireplace took a strong fancy to him and offered him Smith's old snoozing place. Which Mr. Billing, being temporarily without friends, was very glad of, and slept there comfortably till, in one of the old man's dreadful twitchy nightmares, his head was stove in by the old man's chained wrists.

Naturally, a great fuss was made—and it was strongly urged that the old man be sent to Bedlam as being a danger to himself and other prisoners. But he never went, for (and not for the first time) his son—to whom the State was much obliged—pleaded powerfully and successfully for his father to remain in the Stone Hall. His son was Mr. Jones, the hangman . . . so the State could scarce refuse *him* . . .

For a while, Smith and Mr. Mansfield wondered uneasily if this strange and violent incident would affect Miss Mansfield—considering her one-time regard for the lying attorney. But Miss Mansfield was well out of that wood—and indeed, out of the wood that had shadowed most of her life.

For Smith, staying as he did in Vine Street, had become so much Mr. Mansfield's companion and friend that the tempestuous young lady found herself—as often as not—quite unnecessary. She was able to go out and about in the Town, where, by an extraordinary coincidence, a likeable young gentleman from Sussex (though neither of them suspected it at first), had been waiting for her all of his life.

So Smith, despite his independence of pocket and spirit, has stayed on in Vine Street as firmly and cheerfully and contentedly as only a truly free spirit could have done. Nothing holds him but affection: and nothing feeds this affection so much as the deep understanding of his own fair situation in his blind friend's dark world.

Sometimes, of a late afternoon, the pair of them go out together and stroll as far as Golden Square, where Smith tells Mr. Mansfield how fine and prosperous a certain Establishment is looking these days. Then they go inside it, and Miss Bridget and Miss Fanny are pleased and charmed to serve them with chocolate. (Gin? The very idea! We are dealing now with ladies!) Then they go out again, and Smith looks up at their shop sign with a grin.

Miss Bridget and Miss Fanny
Court Dressmakers

He nudges Mr. Mansfield in the ribs.

" 'Oo's to know at the Court they was makers for was the Criminal one at Old Bailey?"

And from their fine bay window, the sisters smile and

wave and watch their neat, small brother and his grand and gentle friend, walk side by side along the Square, till at last they take the corner and are lost from sight.

But now the sun goes down and the air darkens. A wind sets in and clouds swing across the sky. Miss Fanny looks out somewhat sadly and dabs at her eyes with a piece of fine lace. She is thinking of Lord Tom and his glittering ways. But then she looks northward and sighs and smiles. For Lord Tom sleeps in a neat grave at the top of Highgate Hill, overlooking the Finchley Common. Nothing would have pleased him better . . . for from there 'tis but a ghost's step to visit with Bob Bellamy and go a-riding the night wind with Turpin, Robinson, and Duval. A splendid and gallant company!

THE END